Ocean's War

DEMELZA CARLTON

DEDICATION

With thanks to the Katharine Susannah Prichard Writers Centre – without their Fellowship, this book (and the Siren of War series) might never have been finished.

One

When war finally came to our shores, it even took me by surprise.

"What are they building on Pulu Keeling, Mama?" Apalala asked.

There were no human structures on Pulu Keeling, which was why we used it as a birthing ground and a nursery for our children. Pasting a smile on my face, I said, "I do not know. Show me, and perhaps I will be able to tell you."

We swam up to the beach, swapped our tails for legs, and she led me into the jungle. A white, sandy strip marked our path, dimpled with many, many footprints of those who had come here before us, and recently, too, for the jungle jealously guarded its territory and would have retaken it if time had allowed.

Perhaps a hunting party had been here from Home Island, to collect seabirds and coconuts. If so, they'd likely have built a simple atap shelter of four sturdy poles with a coconut fibre roof, like the ones on South Island. But as we emerged from the jungle onto the shore of the lagoon, I knew no hunter had built these.

At first, I thought I was looking at the steam boiler from the *Windsor* shipwreck, and wondered how such a huge ship could have been wrecked in this land-locked lagoon, but as we approached closer still, staring up at the steel structures that were easily three times as tall as that old boiler, my memories darted back to Flying Fish Cove, and the fuel tanks there.

For these were not boilers or engines but enormous metal drums holding the foul-smelling liquid that fuelled the machines of commerce, and of war. They stank of paint as well as fuel, for someone had thought to coat the shiny metal with a rough coat of green, as if that could hide them in the jungle. Perhaps if the trees grew close enough, it might work.

A ladder ran up the side, inviting me to scale it.

"Stay here," I told Apalala, and began to climb.

"What are you doing, Mama? What can you see up there?" Apalala asked, bouncing around in her excitement. She was more confident on her legs than I had been at her age. One day, when she was old enough, that would stand her in good stead among humans.

Now, I felt the most powerful urge to run with her to the sea, and dive into the darkest depths, swimming as far as I could away from all things human, until we were safe.

But William had been right – we would not be safe. Not as long as humans had a way to guide ships beneath the waves.

I reached the top of the tank, and unscrewed the lid. It was full of fuel, all right, but not the thick, inky diesel that had filled the tanks in the port in Flying Fish Cove. No, this could have been water, if not for the sharp smell, more like the petroleum that had fuelled my motorcycle. But a tank this size would have filled a hundred or maybe even a thousand Triumphs – more motorcycles than I'd ever seen. Pulu Keeling had never seen one motorcycle, let alone a hundred.

This wasn't right.

I climbed down again.

"What are they, Mama? What did you see?" she persisted.

At her age, I had seen the Battle of Cocos, seen men die amid screeching, screaming metal in the heat of battle I had wrought. Apalala was innocent of such violence, and I wish I'd believed in Aunt Merry's God, that I might pray to him that she would retain such innocence for many years yet.

For how could I tell my wondering child that what I saw was darkness coming, heralded by the stench of death, and the keening scream that I knew was only the wind now, but would be so much more soon enough.

"I don't know, my darling, but I will ask the soldiers on Direction Island. They will know," I said, and led her back to the sea.

Two

Ceylonese soldiers had taken up residence on both Direction Island and Horsburgh Island, manning the newly installed guns and practicing running from the buildings to the hastily dug trenches on the beaches that filled with water every high tide. Despite all the drills, even they did not seem to believe war was coming – they filled their helmets with hermit crabs to use as bait, and spent most of their time fishing.

They knew little about the people of Home Island, and when I approached the cable station in a borrowed dress, they took me for one of the Clunies-Ross family. My time as a Mem on Christmas Island had taught me how to present the image they expected to see, with my ramrod straight spine and imperious expression.

I asked to see the man in charge, and I was greeted promptly by a dark-haired captain who looked more than a little apprehensive.

If the sight of a prim English miss made him nervous, water help him if he knew what I really was, with the power of the Indian Ocean at my command.

I hid my smile and let him see my concern instead. "A hunting party has found petrol tanks on North Keeling Island, close to the lagoon," I said. "Full tanks."

The man's face paled until it appeared pasty grey, like a dead fish. "That's not possible."

I drew myself up. "I assure you it is. I have seen them with my own eyes, and when I opened the tanks, I saw they were full."

The captain swallowed. "What sort of fuel did you see? Can you tell me?"

I gave him a tight smile. "It looked and smelled like motor spirit. The sort you use in a motor car, or a motorcycle."

He swore under his breath. Too quiet for a human girl to hear him, but I had no trouble. "Or in an aeroplane."

I blinked. The flying boats that landed in the lagoon used motor spirit, too? The pieces fell into place in his head at the same time they clicked in mine.

Pulu Keeling with its inland lagoon was the perfect place to land flying boats. A protected harbour, so secret most people didn't even know the island existed.

"Please thank your father for this information. We will go to North Keeling Island at once, and destroy the tanks before the enemy can use them."

My heart sank. Part of me had hoped that the tanks were built by our soldiers, and not the Japanese troops moving deeper and deeper into Asia. If they weren't ours...they were supplies for a war that was about to spill over into our little piece of paradise.

It was three days before the weather was favourable for a voyage to Pulu Keeling, and I watched the ship head north with a heavy heart. By nightfall, a thick column of black smoke sat on the northern horizon, and I knew the war had begun.

According to the human calendar, this was the fifth day of September, 1941. That was the day my vigil began. It would be almost four years before it ended, and our world would change more than I believed possible.

Three

I haunted the waters around Direction Island, often sitting on the sands of Pulu Beras, across the coral gardens humans called The Gap, where the sounds of the radio floated on the wind. At first, the reports were about a war in far-away Europe, and I began to wonder if William was wrong.

By December, new names rode the radio

waves. Pearl Harbor and the Philippines, Hong Kong and Thailand, and then Malaya. Radio Tokyo announced each victory with a glee uncharacteristic of the Japanese people I'd known on Christmas Island. But if they were to be believed, then William was right. It was only a matter of time before Singapore fell, and, after that, Australia, the radio announcers boasted.

Was nowhere in the world safe?

I glimpsed Sephira in the water, closer to the human-inhabited island than she was permitted to be. I opened my mouth to order her away.

"Is it true? Is Singapore in danger?" she asked.

If you could believe what the Japanese radio announcers said… "Yes, I believe so," I said.

"Then you must help me. I swore to my mother, who swore to my father, that we would preserve his treasures in Singapore. A man named Ruffles has them, in safe keeping, but if Singapore is to fall, then I must go there to retrieve his chest of treasures."

I searched her face, looking for some sign that she was lying, or at least trying to trick me, but her desperation seemed genuine. "Dubhan left treasure with Sir Stamford Raffles? He died a long time ago. I doubt he's protecting anything now."

Sephira shook her head. "No, Mother said it was in Singapore still. In his hotel."

"He left something at the Raffles Hotel?" It was a high-class British establishment, though not as high a standard as the Adelphi, but good enough. The Raffles Hotel staff would likely have kept whatever it was, even if none of the current owners knew why.

"With the Ruffles man. We must preserve it. I promised." She looked up at me, her eyes imploring. "Please, Matriarch Sirena. His treasures come from the Atlantic, for he was one of the first of our kind to colonise the Indian Ocean. He was the last dragon, and your grandfather. He had secrets only his descendants may know. I cannot let his most precious possessions fall into the hands of humans who will destroy them."

Based on what I'd heard of the conquerors' behaviour in China and other places, they'd most likely steal anything of value, to further fuel their war efforts. Whatever Dubhan's treasure might be, it could not be left in Singapore any more.

I sighed. "Fine. We will leave in the morning."

She reared back. "But you cannot go, surely. As Matriarch and a member of the Council…"

I waved her into silence. "I will tell them what I intend to do, and we shall go in the morning. Me because he is my ancestor, and I am the Matriarch of my line, and you because…well, you know more about this than I do. Meet me here at dawn, and we will go to Singapore together."

She looked like she wanted to argue, but I didn't wait to hear it. Instead, I swam away, to convene a Council meeting and to see to my daughters' safety while I was away.

Four

"…I do not know how long it will take to secure my grandfather's property, but I will return as soon as I can, so that I may report on this human war, and what it means for us." I took a deep breath, letting my gaze sweep around the council chamber, touching each of the elders in turn. "If the war should reach you before I return…"

"We shall hide in the deeps, as we have every time humans threaten our people," Thanh said with quiet confidence.

The others began to nod.

"And if it is not enough? With their submarine ships, they might follow you," I said. "If they do, what then?"

"No man has found us in the depths before, and no man will," Thanh said, but she sounded less sure. Her expression was firm, though, as though she clung desperately to this hope, for she did not know what else to do, other than what had always been done.

If I had believed in Merry's god, I would have prayed that Thanh was correct. For Maria and Apalala would be with them, and they would share their fate. I'd lost Maria once and I could not bear to do so again. As for Apalala…she was all I had left of William. I would sink every ship in the sea before I let a human take her from me.

"You should stay with us. With the power of your voice, we will be safer together,"

Shyama said, touching my arm. Her eyes told me she could reach my thoughts from my expression.

I shook her off. "And lose what the last dragon took such pains to preserve for us? No, I must go after Dubhan's treasure, and see to its safety. I will not let our heritage be lost to some petty human conflict. I will go in haste, so that I may return in time to take to the depths with you, when the time comes."

More nodding. For a council of war, we sure were agreeable. Perhaps if humans could reach a consensus so easily, they would not be fighting this pointless war.

But humans were not the people of the ocean's gift, so while we got along beneath the surface, they warred above.

Five

Apalala's seagrass hammock hung beside mine, for she was too big to share with me any more, but she awoke with the sun, as I did.

"Will you bring me back a gift from Singapore?" she asked eagerly, for I had told her many stories about my shopping trips with William. "Maybe a book that I can read?"

Books would not be a bad idea. Our

children needed to learn to better blend in with humans, and letters carved into the sand were no substitute for pen and paper and real books.

"If I can, I will bring a boatload of books home with me," I promised, for I would need a boat to carry Dubhan's treasure here. He'd left it on land, which meant it could not be hidden beneath the waves.

"Yes!" Apalala corkscrewed out of her hammock, doing a little dance around me as I readied myself for the journey.

When I met Sephira, I found Maria there, too.

"Have you come to wish me a good journey?" I asked her.

Maria shook her head, then shot a glance at Sephira. "I am here so that I might come with you. I am old enough to go ashore and join with a man, so that I might be recognised by the council as an adult."

This was Sephira's doing, I was sure of it. Maria was the same age I'd been when I'd met

William, and old enough to be fertile, but there was no need for her to go ashore so young. No need for her to go ashore ever, for I knew Apalala and not Maria would succeed me as the Gold elder when I left the council, and neither would need to for a century at least.

"No, you will not come with me. You will not go ashore yet," I said.

"But, Mother, when you were my age..." she began.

I whirled. "When I was your age, your grandmother had exiled me from our people, for no crime at all, and I struggled mightily to merely survive on land, in the hope that one day I might come home. One day, if you wish, you will go ashore, and you may find a man you wish to join with. But not now, with war on the horizon, and danger in the water as well as on land. We will discuss this when I return, and not before."

Maria shot a beseeching look at Sephira, who shook her head the tiniest bit.

I knew it had been her doing.

Maria ducked her head. "Yes, Mother." She swam away.

I stared after her for a moment. I would not have submitted so readily, but then, neither of my daughters was as turbulent as I had been as a child. For a split second, I almost felt sorry for Sephira, for having to deal with my adolescent self. Then I remembered how she had betrayed me, the ruin she had wrought in William's life and in mine, as well as in Maria's, and all sympathy vanished.

"Come. We are needed in Singapore," I said, gesturing for Sephira to follow me.

Wordlessly, we went.

Six

The Singapore we arrived at was not the city from my memories with William. The streets were packed with soldiers instead of locals, and while they still seethed with chaos, it was not the same. The locals had moved with purpose, something the soldiers seemed to have lost.

The sound of artillery fire in the distance had many of them cowering, hiding their heads in their hands as if to shut out the sound of the very war they'd signed up to fight.

The Adelphi Hotel still stood, and I longed to go inside and book a room, to see if my memories of my time here with William had left a stamp on the place.

But an agonized scream brought my thoughts back to the immediacy of the present. It was a man's scream, as he was unloaded from the back of a truck, then carried on a stretcher into the cathedral across from the hotel.

The cathedral's green lawns were a war zone of their own — narrow trenches were even now being dug.

Did the army mean to make a stand here? I might not be a military strategist, but even I could see the insanity of such a thing. Any men who tried to man these trenches would surely die.

I realized my mistake only a moment later, when another stretcher came out…carrying a corpse. Then the purpose of the trenches became clear. They were graves for the dead.

We would join them if we didn't leave the city soon. Merry would have called it a miracle we'd arrived in time.

I nudged Sephira. "Best we get what we came for, and go," I said in our tongue.

She didn't say anything, and I paused to look closely at her. Between her wide eyes and pale face as she took in our surroundings, she looked as scared as any of the soldiers.

For the first time, I wondered if I hadn't been the only one to have nightmares after the *Emden* sank. For years, I'd dreamed about men screaming as I killed them. Even William had witnessed a few of my nightmares.

Mother had lost a daughter that day, as well as a patient.

Today was a different day, and I intended to lose nobody.

"Where must we go for these things of your father's?" I asked.

"A…bank," Sephira said slowly, stumbling over the unfamiliar words. "Mother brought them from Batavia to a bank in Ruffles' city. My father told her that people do not stay conquered for ever. One day, they rise up, and take back what's theirs."

I opened my mouth to snap that this place belonged to neither the British or the Japanese, though both seemed happy to fight over it. Fools, the lot of them, and I'd be more foolish still if I stopped to explain this human conflict to Sephira.

"Show me," was all I said.

She found the bank easily enough, but the place was full of people trying to take all their money with them as they fled the country.

The bank, however, had run out of ready cash, or so the staff told people, over and over, for they did not want to listen. No, they wanted what was theirs.

As did I.

I pushed through the crowd to one of the tellers.

He looked tired. "Miss, we have no money left – "

I hushed him. "I am here to collect a box which I believe my grandfather left in your strongroom. A box under the name of Dubhan Black."

He sagged in relief. "I'll get it for you directly, miss!"

It took three men to bring the box back, for it was big enough to fit a man inside. Water only knew what was inside it, though I could feel the curiosity coming off the men in waves. They'd kept this box for a century, and finally someone had come to claim it.

I was in no mood to satisfy idle curiosity. Theirs, or my own. "Thank you. We'll be off, then."

The men did not let go of the box. "We'll carry it out to your car, miss."

I wanted to protest, but I bit back my words as I realized how many eyes were upon us. Greedy gazes, assessing the size of the box and how much money it might contain. Maybe none, I wanted to tell them, but they were beyond anything I might say. Panic and fear gripped them in its own siren song – a song so strong, I could not win against it.

The street outside was full of cars, travelling so slowly that flagging one down should be easy enough. I raised a hand to get a driver's attention.

A plane screamed down the street, spitting bullets, followed by a second one, shooting at the first.

Standing in the bank's ornate doorway, we'd been sheltered from the rain of death, but the cars in the street had not been so lucky. And the people outside…even less.

A car with a blood-splashed windscreen veered left, crashing into another car, before it caught fire. I saw a figure slumped over the steering wheel, unmoving, before flames leaped to the second car, too.

A third plane appeared, dropping something onto a building down the street. A moment later, it exploded, throwing great blocks of stone into the street, on top of the crashed cars.

The road was well and truly blocked – no car could make it through. We would have to go on foot.

I reached for one handle of the trunk. "We'll take it from here," I told the men. I gestured for Sephira to take the other handle, and she did.

I swallowed, tasting ash in the back of my throat. Ash from the burning bodies, or the building that had been blown up? I did not know, and I'm not sure I wanted to.

"We need to go," I said, heading for the harbour.

Seven

I had never thought to see the fall of a human city, and as I looked around me, trying to judge where the next bombs would fall so that I might choose a path as far from them as possible, I heartily wished we hadn't timed our visit so as to see the fall of this one.

Bombs fell, bits of buildings fell, planes fell from the sky, screams fell on deaf ears, before suitcases dropped from hands that had held them so tight…until their owners had fallen for the final time, casualties to the rain of death from skies. The only thing that seemed to rise was dust, from buildings and bodies, clouding the air and hiding a little of the horror. Horror we could still hear, though the sounds were growing fainter.

Either there was no one left to scream, or the bombing had fallen behind us.

Ships loomed out of the fog, strange skeletons missing their metal skins. This was the shipyard, where half-built vessels both old and new waited in hope that they might kiss the sea soon. It was curiously untouched, as if the Japanese planes bombing buildings had decided these hulks weren't worth the trouble. Or perhaps they wished to repair their own ships here when the battle was done.

We needed to be well on their way before that happened.

A larger shape loomed out of the fog, feeling familiar. I blinked, barely believing my eyes. But they told the truth – before me lay the *SS Islander*, the very same vessel William had wanted me to sail on, the day he'd died. She was whole, without a single hole marring her hull. She could sail, if she could be put back in the water.

Perhaps it was time to give William his wish, even if it was eight years too late.

I dropped my end of the trunk, telling Sephira to stay with it. I waited until I saw her nod before climbing up the nearest ladder to the deck.

We'd have to winch the trunk aboard, I decided, heading for the winch. I'd seen it used often enough – surely I could figure out how to make it work.

It took several long minutes before I managed to get the engine to cough into life, and swung the cable and sling over the side.

"Put it in the sling, and I'll lift it up here," I called. It was too heavy, I thought. I'd need to go down to help her.

To my surprise, she hefted the box into the

sling herself, her arm muscles straining as they bulged beneath her borrowed dress.

Perhaps not. Maybe I needed to remember my own strength. Perhaps it was being back in a human city that made me think like a weak, human woman again.

I hauled the box up with the winch, then swung it onto the deck.

Sephira climbed up the ladder, and I found her beside me as I crouched down before the box. I don't know who wanted to see inside it more – her or me.

A large padlock secured the lid, or it had until some piece of flying debris had bent the lock almost double. Now, all it took was a bit of twisting and turning before I dropped the broken lock onto the deck. The lid was stiff, and the hinges screeched a protest as I forced them to open in what might have been the first time in a century. Longer, perhaps.

Sephira drew in a breath as I leaned forward to lift the yellowed sailcloth. The chest was filled with papers. Books and loose sheets, all wrapped in a piece of sailcloth that must have come from a huge, old sailing vessel of some kind. I pulled out one of the books, the aged leather cracking beneath even my delicate touch, and opened it.

Page after page of strange symbols met my eyes, none of which I recognised.

"What does it say?" Sephira asked.

I dropped the book back in the box and closed the lid. "I have no idea. It's in some sort of code, or a language I don't understand. A complete waste of time. We should just leave it here and swim away."

Sephira caught my arm. "No! We can't leave it. It must be preserved. We must take it to some human place where it will be safe."

"In other words, as far from here as possible." I scanned the ship. "The *Islander* looks seaworthy. If we could get her into the water, I could sail her somewhere safe." It was bigger than the fishing boats I'd sailed in Fremantle and the Abrolhos, but the principles were the same, surely. As long as there was fuel enough to keep the engine going, a ship couldn't be much harder to sail than a lugger.

An almighty crash sounded from the wall surrounding the shipyard. Water spurted from where the prow of a ship had crashed through. While I watched, the prow lifted, angling upward as if screaming its defiance to the sky before it slid into the water, beneath the surface. Seawater gushed through the hole it had left behind, flooding the shipyard.

The *Islander* shifted beneath us, aroused by the caress of water around her hull. A feeling I knew well.

"What in damnation do you think you're doing?"

The red-faced man raced onto the deck, a picture of panic in his rumpled uniform.

Though age had softened his waistline and added lines to his face, I recognised him as the First Officer William had fought on his first voyage to Christmas Island.

A man who owed William a favour, which my late husband had never had a chance to collect.

"We're leaving before the rest of the city falls down around our ears," I said.

"Look, lady, I don't know who you think you are, but – "

"I'm Maria McGregor. William McGregor's wife and widow. You owed my husband a debt."

He shook his head violently. "McGregor's dead. He took his secrets to the grave."

"But not before he told me what you did."

I held his gaze, not willing to give in to the bully who knew I was right.

His shoulders slumped, defeated.

"We're taking the *Islander*, and leaving Singapore," I said.

He snorted. "We do that, and we're dead. Have you seen what's happening out in the harbour?"

I lifted my head to look.

The Japanese planes might have turned the city to dust, but they'd turned the harbour into soup. It was the Battle of Cocos between the

Sydney and the *Emden* again, magnified a thousandfold.

Bodies and broken ships floated in a growing pool of oil and fuel, calming the harbour waters that should have been churned into frothing panic.

Smaller boats – local fishing vessels, for the most part – moved with purpose between the ships and lifeboats, saving those they could, while the planes overhead ignored them. But for every body that scrambled from lifeboat to rescue vessel, another three were rolled over the side, to join the other corpses in the harbour.

This was what war historians called a blood bath, where the waters ran red and black instead of life-giving blue.

I swallowed back bile. How humans could do such things to one another, I did not know. But I had no desire to swim through that water now.

"We're dead if we stay," I said.

He fought back panic – he knew the truth in

my words, though he refused to admit it. "We'll have a better chance if we leave at night. It'll give me a chance to go get the captain and the rest of the crew. Can't sail this tub without a crew, no matter who your husband is."

I nodded. "You have until midnight to collect what crew you can. Then we leave – with or without you."

He muttered something that definitely wasn't complimentary under his breath, before heading over the side.

Come midnight, we'd see who was crazy – but I was willing to bet this man would be keeping me company as we headed out of the harbour.

Eight

At close to ten, a party approached the *Islander*. Sephira and the box were stowed away comfortably in a cabin, and I'd claimed the one beside it, wishing I'd had even one of the trunks of clothes or books I'd bought with William when we'd last come to Singapore. Or William himself, to command these men with the kind of assurance I couldn't summon for the life of me.

I'd found a hold full of supplies, a galley filled with food, and fuel tanks that were far from empty. I only hoped it would be enough. If it wasn't…well, at least we wouldn't starve, for the ocean would provide. But it had been a long time since I'd cooked anything, and even then it had not been with the electrical appliances that filled the *Islander*'s galley.

I cocked a pistol I'd found in the captain's cabin, pointing it at the newcomers. "Who are you?" I demanded.

"It's us, Mrs McGregor," came the First Officer's voice.

I backed up, giving them space to board the ship, scanning the faces for Captain Smith. "Where's Captain Smith?" I demanded.

"His landlady said he'd been taken ill, but she couldn't tell me which hospital he'd gone to. Took me half the night to find him, and he said to go without him. Too sick to move, he said."

Slowly, I nodded. Better that he stay here

and recover as a prisoner of war than come with us and risk his life. Humans had rules about such things, though I could not recall them clearly. Something about putting a big red cross on things meant medical supplies and wounded men, who were not to be attacked.

"Who's going to be captain, then?" I asked.

He grinned. "Oh, I'm sure that'll be you, Mrs McGregor. Your orders, ma'am?"

It was all a big joke to him, then, was it?

Fine.

"Get this ship ready to go. We leave at midnight, or as soon as we're ready. I want to be well clear of Keppel Harbour before sunrise."

He sketched a mocking salute. "Yes, ma'am."

To his credit, he and his men had us moving shortly after eleven, which appeared to be the perfect time to avoid being bombed from the air, for not a plane could be heard or seen as the *Islander* made her ponderous way through the debris-choked harbour.

A heavy rain shower had cleared away the smoke, and from my place on the lightless bridge, I could see clear across the harbour. Of course, it was all different on the surface, where you couldn't see the mines and sandbars and sunken ships. But, to his credit, the First Officer had navigated this harbour many times, and he managed to take the *Islander* safely between most of the hazards. The exception was a sunken patrol vessel, sheared in two by aerial bombing earlier in the afternoon, that floated just below the surface, ready to cut her jagged teeth on any vessel unfortunate enough to arrive within reach.

Metal scraped on metal as her sheared-off side encountered the *Islander*'s hull, but the *Islander* had been built to withstand more than the merchant and military vessels that hadn't made it out of Keppel Harbour. The scraping sound ceased and the *Islander* steamed serenely on.

I admit to making a mad dash for the lower levels, to see what damage had been done, fearing to see this ship sink like the *Trevessa*, but I was surprised to see the ship was still sound.

When the sun rose, I was surprised to see the ocean was blue again – we were clear of the debris field, though we could hear both ships and bombers in the area.

"Now we're out of the harbour, Captain, where do you suggest we go?" the First Officer asked.

I wished I knew. Fremantle was where William had wanted me to go, swearing it was safe, but with my daughters still at Cocos, it made more sense to head toward them. Then again, Cocos had already proven to be close enough to British territories for the war to reach there. A single bomber could take out all the Cocos settlement. Our box of coded papers might not be safe at Cocos, either.

Christmas Island…William had been adamant that it was far from safe, wanting me as far from it as possible. The British forces had gone to regroup at Batavia, and the

Japanese troops would surely follow. Christmas Island was close enough to Batavia that the Japanese vessels might decide to take Christmas Island first, and use it as their base for taking Batavia. But they had Singapore, or they would soon, so why would they want Batavia, too?

They wanted the phosphate at Christmas Island. Why pay for something when you could conquer the island and have it all for yourself?

Fremantle, or some other West Australian port, seemed the safest bet, but I'd seen enough Australian troops in Singapore to wonder what sort of defences they'd left at home. Then again, even if all the Australian soldiers made it home, they could scarcely defend their whole coastline with such small numbers.

What would William have said?

He would have trusted his men to know their jobs. He would not have needed to tell them what to do.

I swallowed. "What do you suggest?"

"We're a week overdue, picking up the last evacuees from Christmas Island. I took the rest to Singapore, but they're back aboard, or at least the ones I could find are."

More passengers. I hadn't spotted them among the crew, but then again, if they were islanders, even the privileged wives like I once was, they'd be as familiar with this ship as any of the crew.

I nodded, once. "Why did you stay in Singapore, instead of returning to Christmas Island?"

He shrugged. "We were supposed to have an anti-aircraft gun fitted to the ship. We waited in drydock for a week, every day, hearing the same promises that the gun was on the way, but it never came. Probably captured or blown up, now, and we're out here unarmed."

A dark mood settled over him, like the cloud that had obscured Keppel Harbour the day we left. Now, just like then, I chose not to venture into it.

"Wake me when we're close to Sunda Strait," I instructed.

So dark was his mood that he scarcely showed his surprise that I knew our course.

I slept, I woke, I walked the decks, I sought something to eat in the galley where there fortunately was a cook who knew his way around the kitchen, and I returned to the bridge, where I watched the First Officer steer a steady course until I felt confident enough to take a watch myself.

When I announced my intention, he muttered a bit about how we were all going to die anyway, before surrendering the bridge to me.

I might be a siren, but I did not sink the ship. Not that first watch, nor any of the others thereafter. I was a captain in more than just mocking nickname.

We maintained radio silence, but the Japanese had no such restrictions, occupying the radio channels until I opened my mouth to tell the First Officer to turn it off.

"They're boasting about the ships they've sunk, arguing whether a lifeboat can be considered a ship, if it had the whole crew of a merchant vessel clinging to it. They're picking off the survivors as they flee to Batavia."

I swallowed and nodded, not trusting my voice to respond. Human atrocities were beyond my comprehension, even when I'd witnessed them as a child. How they could do such things to one another…

Then it dawned on me – the First Officer spoke Japanese. "Are there any of their ships ahead of us, guarding Sunda Strait?" I asked.

Anywhere else, we might sail around them, but that particular passage was the shortest route to Christmas Island, and it lay just past Batavia.

"None that are willing to say so over the radio."

No, they wouldn't announce it, would they? They'd lie in wait, so that they might drive the survivors away from Batavia and into the arms of what was likely to be a waiting fleet.

"We refuel at Batavia, then, and wait until nightfall to negotiate the Straits," I instructed.

This time his, "Yes, Captain," seemed more of an automatic response than an attempt to mock me. I hid my smile.

Nine

"There is a submarine following us," Sephira announced, stepping onto the bridge as if she belonged there, while we were refuelling at Batavia.

The First Officer moved to shoo her out, insisting passengers did not belong on the bridge, but I halted him.

"How long?" I asked.

She considered for a moment. "Since a few hours after we left the city. They were hiding in the harbour when we left, and they have not surfaced. They're waiting just outside the harbour now, so I went to take a look." Which explained why her hair was wet. At least she'd remembered to don clothes after her swim.

"Japanese, then?" I asked, already knowing the answer.

She shrugged. "It sounds the same as all the others we've seen and heard. What other kind are there?"

My heart sank, but I did my best not to let it show. If only one nation owned submarines, then they would have the advantage in the water. Then again, if other nations had had submarines, why had they not sent them to Singapore?

I nodded. "Thank you." Then I dismissed her.

Not that you would have thought so, from the proud, disdainful look she gave the First Officer as she waltzed out the door, for all the world as if she wanted to seduce the man. Maybe she did.

"What did she say?" he asked.

I considered lying, simply saying she'd said she didn't like him, which her body language had made abundantly clear, but in the end, I chose the truth. Sort of.

"There's a submarine following us. She's seen it, so she knows it's the same one," I said. "It didn't come into the harbour, she says."

"Then hopefully it won't see us leave later," he said.

There was little more we could do but hope. With no weapons — aside from Sephira and I, and we were little use against a ship running at full steam, too far away to hear our song.

Night fell, bringing darkness faster than any dropped bomb, and with it the urge to go. Intuition had served me well in the past, and I didn't intend to ignore it now.

"We have enough fuel. Time to go," I said.

"But we're not full!" the First Officer protested.

"We have more than enough fuel to get us to Fremantle. We leave now." I stepped up to the helm.

Guiding the *Islander* out of Batavia harbour in the dark with all our lights extinguished was hardly a challenge for me. I knew these waters, better than any human, and I could see further than they could in the dark, too. As we headed into Sunda Strait, I listened for the telltale hum of the submarine following us, but the ocean was silent.

They were waiting for us outside the Strait, a flotilla of warships that weren't blocking the way, but were ready to shoot any craft that came through.

The radio blared into life, unleashing a barrage of Japanese that I could not follow.

The First Officer appeared at my side, his face ashen as he reached for the radio. He snapped out a response. Silence, then a rapid question, to which he answered with the same syllables. Their answer seemed to dismiss him.

"What did they say? What did YOU say?" I

demanded.

"They asked if we had secured the ship, and were proceeding to Christmas Island. I told them yes."

"And after you repeated it?"

"They said they would be a day behind us."

My breath hissed out through my teeth. "So William was right, then. He said the Japanese would attack Christmas Island as soon as Singapore fell."

The First Officer's eyes bulged. "McGregor said that? The man's been dead for a decade — how could he have known?"

I shrugged. "William was no fool, as I'm sure you well know. I wish he'd been wrong, but…under the circumstances, I think we should maintain speed until we're out of range, then see if we can head to Flying Fish Cove at full speed, and beat them by more than a day. We need to evacuate everyone we can."

He nodded. "I'll tell the crew. Some of them have family at Christmas Island, and knowing what's coming, they may want to stay."

Stay in a war zone, with a hostile fleet on the horizon? How could…

If it were Cocos, and the family were my girls, I would wish to stay. Perhaps we were not so different after all.

Ten

"Hold, three miles offshore, and prepare for our quarantine officer's launch," came the message from the padang radio station on Christmas Island.

I itched to respond, wanting to ask when and why they'd appointed a quarantine officer. Was there sickness on the island? How much had changed since I'd left?

But we'd observed strict radio silence since leaving the Japanese fleet behind, and we weren't about to break that now.

So I guided us in to the three mile marker, my eyes on the new gun on the cliffs just past the Governor's House. Of course it was trained on us — if that submarine crew had taken control of our vessel as they'd evidently planned, the *Islander* would be a hostile force.

A small boat came alongside, and the First Officer greeted the first man who climbed up as the island's doctor.

A man new to the island, since I'd left. One who wouldn't recognise me.

I slipped into the shadows, as the two men exchanged back slaps and other such manly things.

"What's this nonsense about a quarantine?" the First Officer asked.

The doctor laughed. "Very touchy about illness, the Japanese. If they suspected sickness, they'd be more likely to stand off at a distance, and give us a chance to shoot them before they could shell our harbour. But if you're here to evacuate us, I'm to guide you in and give you the right codes to radio in."

"The Japanese fleet's only a day or two behind us. We'll tie up at the pier, but we'll have to be underway by morning. Tell everyone who doesn't want to be blown to bits like the poor buggers in Singapore to make sure they're aboard before dawn."

"Was it really that bad in Singapore?"

"Worse. Bodies in the road, bodies in the harbour, bits of people all over the place as they send in planes, shooting soldiers and civilians alike. We're lucky to be alive. A submarine followed us to Batavia, but we seem to have shaken them now. If we hadn't, you might be using those guns on the *Islander* now, and my corpse would be floating along with all the rest of them."

The doctor had spotted me, his face flushing red. "Don't you mind, miss, John here will keep you safe from the Japs."

I presumed he meant the First Officer,

whose first name I didn't know.

The First Officer flushed redder than his friend. "This here's Mrs McGregor. William McGregor's widow. She lived on the Island with her husband, until he died. She saw Singapore fall, same as I did. She's headed home to Fremantle, where she has a house. She's the landlady to Captain Smith's wife."

I'd forgotten about that. Merry's house in Fremantle was now the home of Mrs Smith and her children. No matter. I would store my box, and be off before she had time to notice I'd been there.

The doctor coughed. "My condolences, Mrs McGregor. Your husband was a great man."

I thanked him politely, but my words faded into nothingness as we approached the jetty — which looked just the same as when I'd walked along it with William's sister. As if to make it even more familiar still, a figure on a motorcycle raced down the hill, heading down to meet us.

My heart leaped into my throat. William?

My hopes were dashed almost as soon as they'd risen. The motorcycle was running too roughly to be William's, and already brown with rust or mud, I couldn't be sure. The man upon it was thinner than my William, struggling to control the bike as it slipped and slid through the mud.

I didn't wait until the ship was moored before I leaped onto the jetty, and marched up to the man on the motorcycle. The closer I got, the surer I became — the bike wasn't William's, because it was mine. The brand new Triumph William had given me was now a rusted, dented workhorse to the man who had taken his place.

But that didn't stop me from wanting to take it back. Perhaps I could take it to Fremantle, too, and hide it with the box…

"Miss…"

I heard the man's call, but I ignored it. I only had eyes for the cemetery that I'd ignored while I'd lived here. It had sat beside the coffee gardens, a mournful reminder that even in paradise, people died here occasionally.

Where was William? I scanned the stones — there was a fresh marker that looked only a few days old, and beside it, his stone.

I sank to my knees atop where I knew his bones lay. The closest I would ever get to his body again.

"I'm sorry, William. I should never have come here. If it weren't for me, you'd still be living happily, perhaps about to embark on a fresh adventure, seeing as the final evacuation ship is here."

No, William wouldn't have boarded it. He was a fighter, and he would have stayed to defend the island. Probably died, like so many of the soldiers did in Singapore.

But he would have had eight more years, and died a hero, instead of lying in the mud after a motorcycle crash with a crab.

I touched the headstone that bore his name…and mine, too, for he was described as the beloved husband of Maria.

A name I had not used in eight years. Years

I'd stolen from him.

"I'm sorry, William, sorry I stole what should have been yours. I can't change what happened, but I promise you will be the last. The last man I love, and the last man I'll lose."

It had been years since I'd last cried, but I did then, for all that I'd lost the day William died. And to be here again…

"There you are! It's so good to see you, and you haven't aged a day! I'm insanely jealous. You must tell me your secret. Oh, and join us for dinner. If it's to be the last supper on the island before we are forced to flee, then it must be a good one."

I allowed myself to be led away, smiling and nodding at the inane chatter of a woman I vaguely remembered from before.

Eleven

Despite several offers of a bed ashore, I chose to return to my cabin aboard the *Islander* for the night. Perhaps it was silly, but I didn't want to get too accustomed to living on land. Not when I intended to return home as soon as my grandfather's trunk was safely stored. I told myself the bed in my cabin was a necessary evil I would have to endure to keep the secret of my nature from these people who had known me in my old life.

Sephira, of course, had no such qualms — she'd strung up a hammock in the hold beneath the waterline (water only knows where she found it) and refused to sleep anywhere else. Now we'd stopped, I knew she'd take the opportunity to catch fresh fish for breakfast, so I was not surprised to hear the soft splash of her diving overboard in the darkness before dawn.

What I did not expect was to have my cabin door slammed open shortly after, to find her standing there, dripping on the deck.

"The submarine has returned. It's slowing now, moving into position to be ready to shoot this vessel," she said.

"We need to get everyone ashore, where they'll be safe," I said, reaching for my dress.

"No. There are more ships coming, you said. You must take this one to another harbour, and Father's box with you." Sephira's gaze hardened. "This submarine makes war in our ocean. It must be stopped, and I will be the one to stop it."

"I'll help you!" I cried, though I hadn't the first idea how to do it.

"No," she said. "I may not be as powerful a singer as you, but water carries siren song better than air ever could. I will sing until they no longer have the stomach for war." As she met my eyes, I glimpsed the powerful elder she'd once been, before I had taken her place. "Go. Take this ship and its humans to safety. That is what you want, is it not? To save them?"

Water help me, but I did. I might not be one of them, but I could not let stand by and let these people die.

"Do not wait for me. I will see you again, water willing, in the shallow reefs of home."

I raised a hand in farewell, but she did not give me time to say it before she dived over the side.

Full of misgivings, I roused the crew, and told them to make the ship ready to set sail.

The sooner we left here, the sooner I could return home.

I scanned the surface of the sea, but I saw no sign of the submarine. Then a strange cloud of bubbles burst on the surface, at the entrance to the cove. A cloud that moved closer and closer, heading right for us.

Sephira had failed. No siren could take on a submarine by herself.

But human weapons might. The submarine was surely within range of the new guns.

I leaped ashore and sprinted down the jetty, heedless of who saw me. My motorcycle waited outside the offices, begging to be ridden. I kicked it into life, feeling the unfamiliar rumble of a badly tuned bike beneath me before I set off down the road, past the Governor's House, to the raw, new road they'd carved into the cliff face for the guns.

Men stuck their heads out of the buildings as I passed, and I shouted, "There's a submarine in the cove! Shoot it before it gets the *Islander*!"

They spilled out, running in bare feet with half-buttoned shirts, or in some cases, no shirts at all.

They all knew to lose the *Islander* was to lose their connection to the outside world, and supplies to keep them going until the next ship docked.

The boom of the guns firing made my ears ring, so I could no longer hear the submarine. I could not stay here. I had to get back to the *Islander*.

The motorcycle whined as I tried to coax greater speed from it. I did not remember it being this slow when I'd ridden it beside William – years of neglect had taken its toll on the machine. My once beautiful motorcycle was now a piece of junk, fit only to be ridden by those who did not care for the love with which it had been bought. I would not take this ruin with me to Fremantle – I would remember it as it was, when William was alive, and life was rosy and simple.

As it never would be again.

A splash dragged my eyes back to the cove. The submarine had surfaced, not a hundred yards from the *Islander*. A spreading pool of oil calmed the waves, and I feared for the *Islander* even as I ran toward her .

"Are we hit?" I yelled, not breaking stride as I headed for the bridge.

"Not that I can see," the First Officer said, peering at the instruments. "Surely we would have felt it."

Yes, that was true. I'd seen ships shudder when hit, both in Keppel Harbour and during that long ago battle that ended the *Emden*.

"We need to go."

"Yes, Captain. She's ready. I'll tell the men to cast off the lines now."

I surveyed the sea, but the submarine had submerged again, leaving little behind but an oily wake. I strained my ears to hear the sound of its engine, but I could not hear it over the roar of our own.

We steamed out of Flying Fish Cove, my

knuckles white as I gripped the wheel, wishing I had the sort of faith that would allow me to pray to some higher power. A power that could deliver us from the submarine and the other enemy ships on the way.

But Merry had been the one who believed in such things, not me.

I could only hope.

Hope that Sephira would somehow stop the submarine from following us, hope that the ships we'd seen off Sunda Strait would stay away from us, and hope that the *Islander* would reach Fremantle safely, with an additional thirty-four souls aboard who had chosen to tie their fate to mine for this voyage.

Humans looking to me to lead them. If it wasn't such a desperate situation, I might have laughed. As it was, I did my best not to cry.

William would have been proud.

Twelve

A day's sail from Christmas Island, and still no sign of the submarine. I dared to breathe again.

In the past, when I'd sailed on the *Islander*, there had been a clear demarcation between passengers and crew. Now, it was gone. Every passenger took it into his or her head to keep a watch for enemy ships, as did the crew, so any time of the day or night, I would find someone on deck, peering out into the darkness, or watching the waves.

I felt their eyes upon me, too — I made no effort to hide the fact that I shared responsibility for the ship with the First Officer, and the other passengers whispered, not knowing I could hear their words.

But for every emphatic, "I never heard of a woman captain!" there was a more thoughtful, "Well, in times of war…I heard she steered the ship out of Keppel Harbour, dodging planes and bombs and burning boats…"

Most of them hadn't seen the submarine, but the tale soon spread about that, too — that I'd gunned it down myself, before jumping back aboard to take us out of harbour.

I considered denying the rumours, but I'd learned long ago in the Fremantle Fish Markets that such stories of heroism were how they justified their faith. Boys slaying giants, men rising from the dead or making fish multiply…or a woman saving a ship from a submarine. If they followed me as far as

Fremantle, they could have their stories.

Just as long as they didn't guess at the truth. For no one would believe a story about a siren who saved a ship.

Even I laughed quietly to myself at the absurdity of it.

Well, in times of war…

Thirteen

After having the Indian Ocean to ourselves, maintaining radio silence that only added to our isolation, I found Gage Roads, the shipping lane into Fremantle, a rude shock.

So many ships waited to be allowed into the already crowded port that it was nearly three full days we waited for our turn to berth.

And when we did, I could no longer tell

myself that this was merely normal for the busy port of Fremantle, because…it wasn't. Never before had I seen ships moored two abreast, with gangways between them allowing access to the shore, yet here they were two, three, four and even five abreast at some berths.

Our crew and passengers were considered refugees now, for we'd fled both Singapore and Christmas Island. Some had family to take them in, while others dispersed to find lodgings. We were one of the first ships to arrive from Singapore, and there were questions and calls for news from all sides, from soldiers and civilians alike.

We wanted news of our own. Had Christmas Island fallen? Or Batavia? Had the Japanese attacked Australia yet?

But the close lipped soldiers merely shrugged off our questions and repeated their own.

No one knew what was happening in the north, and that knowledge was desperately needed. They'd lost radio contact with Cocos and Christmas Island, too, while we'd sailed in silence.

Then there was the matter of the *Islander*. It belonged to the Christmas Island Phosphate Company, and in part to the Straits Settlements, but as both were possibly under Japanese control, the ship was now considered a captured prize. It would be put to use in the war effort, one of the soldiers assured the First Officer, but what use, he could not say.

I stayed silent now, hoping to avoid notice, for I would not linger here long. Long enough to take my box up the hill to Merry's house, perhaps spend the night on Mrs Smith's back veranda, before heading out to sea again.

My trudge home mirrored the day I'd left Fremantle, when Merry had still lived. Only this time, I was lugging a trunk up the hill to her house, instead of down toward the port.

My house now, though the thought felt alien in my head. My people did not own houses, or any kind of property. Even my grandfather's box of papers was an oddity. An oddity to be preserved, until I had time to investigate them properly, and perhaps learn how to read them.

Fourteen

When I reached Merry's house – I could not yet think of the place as mine – I knocked on the front door twice before pressing my ear to it. Not a sound – there was no one home. The schoolhouse next door was silent, too – perhaps it was school holidays.

I dragged my trunk around to the back, then let it fall to the deck with a satisfying thump. It could stay on the back veranda until I decided where to store it.

It had been more than ten years since I'd last been here, but the spare key was still where Merry had stashed it, tucked beneath the back steps.

I let myself in. Tears pricked at my eyes as I saw Merry's kitchen, almost exactly as she'd left it. My mouth watered at the thought of her mulberry jam, smeared on bread fresh from the baker's, at the end of a shift at the fish markets.

I felt…home.

I shook myself. This had been Maria Speranza's home, not mine. I was Elder Sirena of the Gold line, and my home was a reef full of fish, far to the north.

But I could not resist going deeper into the house. My bedroom was empty of all but the bed, the bare mattress on its timber frame telling me no one slept here any more.

I thought Captain Smith had said he and his wife had three children – did they all sleep in the same room, or had they left?

The room across the hall had two new beds in it, made with the same hospital precision as the staff had done at our house on Christmas Island. Maids were not common here in Perth, but I suppose Mrs Smith might have taught her children to make their beds so. I opened a cupboard, to find it full of army uniforms.

I shook my head. A lot could happen in ten years. Like my own daughter Maria, children grew up. One of her children had evidently moved out of home, while the other two…must have joined the armed forces here. Men as well as ships would be needed to defend Fremantle.

Merry's room, its front windows overlooking the water, had always been her domain. Hers, and hers alone. Yet now I could not resist stepping inside it, to see if anything of her lingered.

The sharp corners on the blankets and sheets here were as far from Merry as one could get. Her washstand was gone, replaced with a desk. The mess of maps and papers upon it was a strong contrast to the regimental precision of the bed.

I pulled one of the maps toward me, to be able to see it better. It appeared to be a map of the port, and several miles of the coastline, but a rough hand had drawn circular symbols at certain points. The highest points, I realised, peering at it more closely. Only then did I look at the writing scrawled along the bottom, which said: Fremantle Fortress Anti Aircraft Gun Installations.

A gasp left my lips. William was wrong. When all these ships had come to Fremantle, seeking shelter, they'd brought the fighting with them. War had come to Fremantle, too.

Fifteen

I hauled the trunk inside the house, hiding it in my empty wardrobe. Then, my mission accomplished, I should have slipped into the harbour and out into open water, to head for home.

But as I watched the hive of activity the harbour had become, I hesitated. To leave now, in broad daylight with so many boats about, someone would be sure to see me. Better to wait until the cover of darkness, and sneak out safely then.

So instead of swimming, like any sensible siren would do, I made myself a pot of tea and sat on the veranda to drink it. I'd never realised what a lovely view of the harbour Merry had from her bedroom window, though Mrs Smith evidently had, setting a chair and table out here where she might watch the ships. Perhaps she'd been keeping watch for her husband, in the *Islander.* I hoped he'd recovered from his illness, and would soon be on his way home.

Just as long as he hadn't become one of the civilian casualties when Singapore fell…

"You there! What are you doing?"

It took me a moment to realise the young soldier was shouting at me.

A very foolish young soldier, if he had to ask such things.

"Drinking tea," I answered, lifting my cup high so that he might see what he'd evidently missed.

He looked irritated. Good. "No, what are you doing at that house?"

"Drinking tea," I repeated.

"You can't do that there, miss. No women allowed in this street, it's too close to the harbour to be safe. Best you go home to your father, miss, where you'll be safe."

I set my cup down carefully, not wanting to break any of Merry's precious china.

"This is my house, and I'll drink what and where I damn well please in it." The shock on his face at my coarse language almost made me laugh. Perhaps I'd spent too long associating with the crew aboard the *Islander* instead of its more delicate-tongued female passengers.

He straightened, stiffening his spine against the blasting he knew he'd receive in response. He had courage, this boy, I'll give him that. "No, miss, you can't. All civilians have been evacuated from this street for their own safety. Soldiers stay here now, to guard the port from enemy ships."

I folded my arms across my chest. "I've

done all the evacuating I intend to. I came by ship from Singapore this morning, and now you're trying to tell me soldiers have stolen my house? What have you done with my tenant, Mrs Smith?"

His eyes widened. This boy had never seen battle, that was certain. Then again, he had little chance of winning against a siren, either. "What did you say your name was, miss?"

"Mrs Maria McGregor, nee Speranza, niece to Merry D'Angelo, who willed this house to me upon her death." I waved my hand imperiously. "Speak to Merry's and my lawyer in the city, a man by the name of Raphael D'Angelo. He'll tell you."

"If he's Italian, miss, he's been interned in one of the camps with all the other aliens."

Half of Fremantle was Italian. Is that where they'd sent them…camps?

"Do you have your passport, miss?" he asked hopefully.

I'd had such a thing, once. Water only knew where it was now. Packed with my things that went aboard the *Islander*, the day William died. After everything that had happened since that day, this silly boy expected me to know where a piece of card had gone?

"I left Singapore with little more than the clothes I was wearing. Which is more than most."

He nodded, though he didn't look happy. "Is there anyone here who might speak for you, say you are who you say you are? Someone who'd recognise you, perhaps?"

Merry would have known me in a moment. Or any of the men from the fish market.

"Ask any fisherman in Fremantle. The men in the fish market would all know me."

Even as the words left my lips, I realised my mistake.

"There's no more fish market in Fremantle, miss. All the Italian fishermen are in the internment camps."

Water, who else did I know in the city? I'd been gone for too many years. Surely there had to be someone else. "Lucy," I blurted out. But

I could not for the life of me remember her last name. "She worked with numbers. An accountant, with the courts. We went out to the Houtman Abrolhos together on the Naturalists Club trip in '30. Her brother was in the Club, too. He started it, I think."

"Stay right there, miss. I'll find her."

The boy ran off.

I had no intention of moving – I still had half a pot of tea to drink. And it wasn't nearly nightfall yet.

The brilliant orange sunset was already sinking into the sea when I heard a woman's voice call my name.

"Maria…is it really you?"

Lucy had aged, but I knew her voice still. She was thinner, too, with the beginnings of wrinkles about her eyes. Whereas age had not touched me.

She flew up the front steps and hugged me. "Aunt Merry said you'd married some man in Ceylon and you lived there now. I wanted to write, but she died before she could give me the address."

Her letters wouldn't have reached me under the sea, but I couldn't tell her that.

"I married William McGregor, a Scottish engineer at the phosphate mine on Christmas Island."

She wrinkled her nose. "Where on Earth is Christmas Island?"

"Far to the north, on the other side of Sunda Strait from Batavia. We'd have to take a ship to Singapore to do our shopping."

"And where is your husband? I'd love to meet him. Is he as handsome as my Giorgio?"

So she was still with the Italian boy she'd fallen in love with at the Abrolhos. I hoped the silly boy had turned into a man during the intervening years.

I didn't want to talk about William. To see the pity and sympathy in her eyes when I told her I'd been widowed again…no, I did not want to cry. Especially with the young soldier watching on the road behind her.

"How is Giorgio?" I asked.

She blushed "Well, he goes by George, now, of course. He joined the army to help save Singapore. Perhaps you saw him while you were there?"

He'd been one of the soldiers in Singapore? My heart sank. "It's a very busy city, and I was more worried about getting out of it than looking for friends from Fremantle while I was there," I said honestly.

"Oh." I'd pricked her little balloon of hope, but she did not let it pop. "If you're here, does that mean he'll be home soon, too?"

"If he's a soldier, he was probably sent to Batavia." If he was still alive.

"Oh."

Capitalising on the lull in our conversation, the soldier stepped in. "So, can you tell me who this is, ma'am?" he asked.

"She's Aunt Merry's niece, Maria. Speranza back then, but McGregor now, I suppose." Lucy gestured at the door. "And this is her house."

The soldier seemed satisfied with that,

though he wasn't happy. "Thank you, ma'am. I have orders to see you safely home now."

Lucy looked alarmed. "But…I haven't seen her for years. We need to talk."

Never had a simple verb held such dread for me, but I managed a smile, all the same.

"You must come into town and meet me for lunch, Maria," she said. Age had given her an assertive air she'd lacked when she was younger. It suited her. "This week, or next, at the latest. I insist."

I nodded. Let her think I was staying here, instead of swimming away as soon as they'd left and I'd rinsed the teapot.

I endured a hug and a kiss from Lucy, clasping her bony shoulders as if she were my dearest friend in all the world. Among humans, she just might be.

And then they were off, her and the boy soldier, leaving me to my solitude. To prepare for my swim.

Sixteen

When darkness fell, I cleaned up the kitchen – not that I'd made much mess, but still – before I locked the door and returned the key to its hiding place. Maybe I'd come back one day, when the war was over and the girls were all grown up, with children of their own. Or I could bring the girls ashore, so they might find fathers for the children they hoped to have.

Now I thought about it, that seemed far more practical than the way I'd done things with Giuseppe, or even William. And it wasn't like living among humans was hard.

But that was for later. Now, the water waited.

The way to the sea was barred by rolls of barbed wire, which caught on my dress and ripped my skirt half to ribbons. Oh well, it wasn't like I'd need clothes where I was going.

"Hey, you, stop!"

Bright light blinded me and I stumbled for the water, blinking furiously until my vision cleared. I slid down the bank in a cascade of soil and stone, before my feet sank into river mud. The waves licked at my toes. I slid beneath them in a moment, making for the depths in the middle of the river channel.

"She went into the water!" I heard someone shout.

The dark surface glowed white, as more than one searchlight turned to splash across the water.

Losing no time, I transformed, relishing the rush of water through my gills. What was left of my dress dragged in the current, but I could take it off later, once I'd reached open water. I powered past the bridge, into the port proper.

The ships all around me cast heavy shadows, hiding me from the lights I'd left behind. The tide was headed out, so I let the current take me. I would need to conserve as much energy as I could for the long swim home.

I closed my eyes, rejoicing in the gentle caress of the ocean, urging me on. This was home, I told myself. The unending roll of waves over the swirling currents beneath, a banquet of fish at my call, and a soft seaweed hammock wherever I chose to lay my head. Home was not tea or jam or pillows or motorcycles.

Home was —

I slammed against an invisible barrier, one that moved with me, even as it barred my way.

A net, my hands told me, just like the shark

net that had once blocked off the swimming baths. But that net had been tarred rope, while the strands of this were unyielding steel. I dove deeper, seeking to swim under it, but the bloody thing was fastened to big concrete blocks on the bottom of the harbour, so new even the local sealife hadn't colonised them yet. It stretched from the northern seawall to the southern one, stopping ships and submarines from entering or leaving the busy port without permission.

And barring the way of one increasingly pissed-off siren.

If I could not swim under or through it, then over I would go, I told myself, swapping my tail for human legs so that I might climb the structure.

Air chilled my fingers before I realised I'd reached the surface, yet the netting stretched further. I climbed all the way out of the water, and still had ten feet to go.

"There she is! She's climbing the submarine net!"

I cursed.

Spotlights drenched me, setting the water droplets aglow as they slid down my skin.

I climbed faster.

"Mrs McGregor, come down to the boat. We'll help you to shore."

I glanced down. The boy from the house sat in a patrol boat beneath me, calling my name.

I closed my eyes.

I could try to sing, to make them all forget me and let me get away, but I wasn't sure how far my voice would carry across the harbour.

Then there was Lucy, and how many other people had this boy told about me?

If I kept climbing, siren song or not, I would have to shed my human life forever and never return. I would lose Merry's house, and all the memories it held. Like I'd lost William and our home at Christmas Island, and my motorcycle, the last gift he'd ever given me…

I swallowed, and began to climb down.

I would go with them, say whatever I had to in order to get out of there, then head down to a beach to swim home. It would be a short delay, no more.

I leaped lightly onto the deck, then straightened to meet the eyes of the boy. He held out a blanket, as though he wished to wrap me up like a child.

"I'm not cold," I snapped, turning away. On a warm March night like this, with only a slight breeze coming off the water, not even a normal human would want a blanket.

"But your dress has been torn to rags, Mrs McGregor." A blush heated his cheeks.

Oh, it was a matter of modesty, that strange human concept where they believed women had to cover up or risk men turning into lustful monsters. I toyed with wanting to tell the boy that I was the monster, capable of driving men to insane levels of lust with just my voice, and I had used it to lure men to their deaths.

But of course I didn't.

I took the blanket and tied it about me like a sarong.

The patrol boat tied up at wharf, and I was marched between a squad of men to the limestone buildings convicts had constructed in the early days of the settlement at Arthur Head. Prison cells had been turned to offices, it seemed, and there were more men guarding them than there had been before.

We reached a closed door and the squad dispersed, leaving me alone with the boy, who still gripped my arm. His hands were bigger than mine, and he'd already started to develop the muscles that might one day make him a formidable man, but to his credit, he chose not to demonstrate the power he believed he held over me. His grip spoke of reassurance, a plea not to run, and perhaps even a whisper of support.

I almost wished he'd dug his fingers into my flesh, trying to mark me into submission, as the message that I was his prisoner sank in.

If he'd been cruel, I might have pulled away. Sung him and the rest of the fort to sleep, and dived off the breakwater into the sea.

Instead, I waited for him to knock on the door, and for the man inside to command us to enter. The boy dropped my arm then, gesturing for me to precede him.

Like William would have.

I swallowed, and stepped inside.

"What is it, Ensign?" The man at the desk didn't even look up.

"We caught this woman trying to swim through the submarine net into the sea, sir. She came on one of the refugee ships that docked this morning. Some of the men suspect she's a spy."

The man scrutinised me for a second. "Young girls don't make good spies. Take her home, Ensign."

"But Sir – "

"I said take her home."

Hesitant fingers crept around my arm. "C'mon, Mrs McGregor, I'll take you home."

The door opened. "Captain Green, there's an update on Cocos. And a report from Broome."

I shook free of the boy's grasp. "What news of Cocos?"

"Mrs McGregor – "

The Captain turned his eyes on me again. "Japanese ships bombarded it today, and Radio Tokyo is reporting that they split the island in two."

My heart stuttered within my chest. They couldn't. They hadn't… I fought to keep calm, and forced out a snort. "Sounds like bullshit to me. Did they say which island? There are dozens. Some of them no one lives on. If it was Pulu Beras, a good wave or a big storm can make it disappear for months before enough sand collects for it to surface again." I met the Captain's gaze and did not look away.

"Are you familiar with the cable station?"

I swallowed. The undersea telegraph cable was the surest path between here and home, for it snaked all the way across the Indian Ocean. "They shelled Direction Island?"

"The cable station staff sent an uncoded signal yesterday to say the cable station had been disabled. Nothing else since."

"I need to go home. My children – " I began.

The Captain waved his hand. "You heard the woman, Ensign. Take her home."

I shrugged the boy off again. "My home, and my children, are at Cocos. Put me on the next ship home."

"Ma'am, in case you haven't noticed, there's a war on. If Japanese ships have taken Cocos, we won't be sending any passenger ships there. Far too dangerous."

I'd endured the voyage once in the *Islander*'s hold, and I would endure it again to see that my children were safe.

"Then a hammock in the hold of one of your warships, for surely you need that cable station – "

"We don't allow women on warships!" the Captain exploded. "Far too dangerous."

I stood my ground. "I sailed the *SS Islander* out of Singapore harbour, with planes bombing ships and streets all around. A submarine followed us to Batavia, but I managed to shake it off and reach Christmas Island safely, in time to notify their gunners to keep a lookout for the sub. They shot it down within the day, and I sailed the *Islander* here, arriving this morning. I've seen plenty of danger on my way here, and I'm willing to risk more, to get home to my children."

The Captain sighed. "Miss, you cannot possibly have done all that alone."

"No. I brought more than thirty refugees with me from Christmas Island, too. Perhaps when your next ship goes to Christmas Island — "

"We lost radio contact with Christmas Island on the 19th, more than two weeks ago."

The day after we left. My heart sank. "Or Batavia — "

"We lost that and the battle of Java Sea last week. We even lost a heavy cruiser of our own, the *Houston*, in that battle. The survivors flew to Broome, and the Japanese followed them. Bombed Broome this morning. Between here and Ceylon, the Indian Ocean belongs to the Japanese, ma'am, until we bring in enough firepower to win it back. So get this woman out of my office, Ensign – I have enough work to do."

Another man burst into the office. "Sir! Japanese submarines sighted up near Cervantes! Bombers on their way to intercept."

"Must be the one I saw off Cottesloe Beach last night, while we were waiting to come into the harbour," I offered. "They were sitting on the surface, with the crew camped out on top, enjoying the dancehall music as they discussed which of the ships to torpedo. They were waiting for orders."

Orders they'd undoubtedly received.

The Captain rose. "Get her out of here, Ensign. Now!"

Cocos. Singapore. Batavia. Christmas Island. And now Fremantle, too?

Despair threatened to drag me under, so I had no strength to resist the boy who lifted me bodily from the Captain's office.

Seventeen

Home again, I did what Merry would have done: I brewed another pot of tea. There was precious little of my Japanese green tea left in the tin, and I didn't like my chances of getting any more soon. I'd watched the cook aboard the *Islander* light the gas stoves in the galley enough times to know what I was doing with this one, though as the gas ignited and scorched the backs of my fingers, I wished the house still had Merry's wood stove.

"Aren't you going to put some clothes on, miss? Mrs McGregor?"

The boy had brought me home, and now he wouldn't leave.

I considered telling him that I spent my summer nights naked, but somehow I thought even that wouldn't get rid of him. I'd evidently missed the Captain ordering him to guard me.

"These are all the clothes I left Singapore with," I said instead.

"Then I must find you something. I think there's a shirt the LT left behind that might fit…" He wandered out of the kitchen, leaving me alone.

Well, not entirely alone. The refrigerator – another appliance I'd seen on the *Islander* – hummed tunelessly in the place where Merry's ice chest had stood. A noisy reminder that the world had changed since I'd chosen to return to the ocean.

An ocean humans were trying to claim, with

their sneaking submarines, shrieking bomber planes, and the bloody aftermath of their battles. My ocean, not theirs.

I had fought my mother and my own people for it, but it had not been enough. I would have to fight these human warmongers, too.

But what could one siren do against an ocean of ships? Oh, I could sink them all, one at a time, sending them down to the depths while I set sharks upon the survivors, but…not everyone deserved to die. Some had taken to the seas to defend their homes from invaders. That made them my allies, surely. Anyone who wanted the war to end so the bodies would stop piling up in the Indian Ocean was my ally, whether they knew it or not.

"Sorry, Mrs McGregor, but this is all I could find. Better than nothing, I suppose. There might be some women's clothes in those boxes in the shed out the back, but this should do you until morning." The boy held out an armful of khaki-coloured cloth, which I reluctantly accepted.

Soldiers' clothes, all of it. I eyed the pants with distaste.

The observant boy didn't miss my expression. "I washed them yesterday, ma'am, at the barracks laundry. They're as clean as can be. I swear I'll look in the shed at first light, to see if there's something more suitable for a lady."

I wished I could tell him it wasn't the pants themselves I didn't like, but the necessity of wearing clothes at all. Pants were just more restrictive than most. I sighed and headed for my old bedroom to dress. The pants were the least of my worries, as it turned out, for the shirt with its stiffly starched collar felt like the sharp edge of a knife against my neck.

My hair had grown since I was last on land, so I braided it back, tying off the end with a ribbon torn from my ruined dress.

When I returned to the kitchen, the boy let out a low whistle. "Ooh, don't you look smart! Just like the AWAS down at the WACA."

I blinked, trying to remember what those

things were. WACA, I finally recalled, was the cricket grounds and sports stadium in Perth, but I'd never heard of the AWAS. Whatever it was, it had likely been built while I was away. Dismissing the gaps in my knowledge, I poured myself another cup of tea.

"Would you like a cup?" I asked the boy.

He wrinkled his nose. "No, though I wouldn't say no to a coffee." He looked hopeful.

Did he expect me to make it? I almost laughed. As Mrs McGregor or a mermaid, I'd never made coffee for a man in my life. "Alas, my cook and both my maids chose to stay at Christmas Island instead of evacuating with the rest of us, so I can't ask them to make any for you." My stomach grumbled as it remembered the delights that had come out of that kitchen. "Or dinner for me."

"We usually go up to the mess at the barracks for our meals, but it's too late for dinner now. Besides, even if you showed up in one of our uniforms, they'd know a mile off you're not one of our men." The boy blushed, unable to meet my eyes.

Yes, the shirt was rather tight across my chest. When I was younger, we'd had undergarments that flattened our breasts instead of emphasising them, like the ones I wore today.

"But we should have some bread and butter. Maybe even some jam, if my uncle hasn't finished it all." He opened the refrigerator and rummaged through the contents.

The clothes, the familiarity with the house and its contents…he lived here, I finally realised. No wonder he'd challenged me for sitting on the veranda.

Over bread, jam, tea and a pot of coffee he made for himself, he told me his story. His name was Tane Green and he'd joined up after Pearl Harbor, determined to fight back. His uncle, one of the officers being sent over to Australia to help set up the submarine base, had requested him, and so he'd come here instead of being assigned a ship. I got the impression he would have preferred serving on a ship or a submarine to being a combination of his uncle's clerk and messenger.

Oh, and he wasn't a soldier. He was an ensign in the United Stated Navy.

When he finally paused for breath, I asked, "Why are you telling me all this, if you think I'm a spy? Loose lips sink ships, or at least that's what the posters say down by the wharf."

He reddened. "I – "

"What's she doing here? I thought I told you to take the girl home! Her home, not ours!"

The Captain took off his hat and glared at Tane.

Tane didn't rise and salute, like I would have expected. Instead, he folded his arms and met the Captain's gaze. "This is our landlady, Uncle. A respectable widow who spent half her life here, before she remarried and moved to some islands up near Ceylon. One who knows the coastline here very well, for she's sailed it herself with some of the local fishermen. The crew of the *Islander* swear she sailed that ship, too, and some say she gunned down the submarine herself. They also said her husband was a staunch Scotsman, the phosphate mine's engineer, and he died before the war."

He'd done his research — likely with Lucy and the crew. He was a smart boy, this one. Except… "You forgot the bit about suspecting I'm a spy," I said dryly, draining my tea.

Tane ignored me. "She swam the length of the harbour, from here to the submarine net, and no one saw her surface. If we'd been there a moment later, I have no doubt she'd have been over the net and seeking passage from one of the ships moored offshore. She's been inside the house, but she didn't take the maps, or even make a copy of them. Her ship waited for three days to enter the harbour — she could have easily swum ashore and done whatever she wanted before swimming back to her ship in that time. She reads, writes and even ran the fish market, according to the locals." He took a deep breath. "I think she'd make you an excellent secretary, Uncle."

Thereby freeing him to go to sea, the way he wanted. Surely his uncle could see through such a transparent ploy?

Yet the Captain merely looked thoughtful.

"Can you use a radio? Do you know Morse code?" he asked.

Between watching William at work at the Padang radio station and spending too much time with the Cable Station staff on Direction Island… "Yes to both," I answered warily.

"Ever work with ciphers?"

"I don't know what those are."

"Ciphers are codes, systems for disguising your communications from the enemy."

"Of course not," I snapped. "The *Islander* is a civilian vessel. We spent the whole voyage under radio silence. The only people who need such things are soldiers and…"

"Spies," Tane finished for me with a smile.

I scowled at him. "I will not be anyone's

secretary. I intend to go home on the first available boat."

The Captain didn't look the slightest bit perturbed. "What if I could promise you a berth on that boat?"

I opened my mouth to refuse, but he held up a hand to stop me.

"Now, hear me out, ma'am. There won't be any boats headed for Cocos until the war's over. Not because it's been bombed but because they've got the cable station up and running again. The Japs don't know, and I aint telling them. They've even got a new name for the despatches, so no one knows Cocos is still operational."

I breathed out a sigh of relief. My girls would be all right.

"Now, I have a problem. Most of our best men are out on patrol. The good ones who aren't…well, they're like my nephew Tane here. Bright and eager, but they wouldn't know a submarine from a shark. The Aussie troops…they've given me fly boys and gunners. They like to shoot, but they don't like to ask questions. Trained it out of them, maybe. Good in a battle, but not so good when a plane sees a submarine and starts shooting. Like when a friendly sub screams out the right code to tell the plane to stand down, and the bomber doesn't notice over the explosions."

The submarine at Cervantes hadn't been Japanese at all, I realised. "Were your men all right?" I asked.

The Captain waved away my concern, but his eyes remained too hard for me to believe he'd made the scenario up. "We all know the risks when we joined up. Everyone dies eventually, but not everyone has the chance to do it for their country."

Empty rhetoric. I wouldn't die for the ocean, for all that it was my home. But I would kill for it.

He cleared his throat. "I need someone I can trust. Someone who will hesitate only long enough to check, before calling in the guns.

Someone who pays attention, and someone who will tell me what's coming for us. Someone who will report to me when something feels wrong."

I folded my arms across my chest. "I won't be your secretary, or your spy."

He acted like he hadn't heard. "I need someone on that island off the coast. There's gun batteries, an aerodrome, nothing for miles around. If anything comes near the harbour, I need someone who'll see it first, and give me time to act. Someone I can trust to know the difference between a Japanese submarine, or an American one."

I had yet to see anything but a Japanese submarine, so that wasn't me. "Why would you trust me? You only met me today. You don't know me."

The Captain smiled, as if he imagined himself a shark about to devour an easy meal.

I commanded sharks as easily as breathing. All I'd have to do would be to open my mouth, and I would control him, too.

But he was right about one thing – I would hesitate long enough to hear what he had to say first. Because I could choose whether he was my ally…or not.

"I know nothing matters to a woman more than her children. I know you want to go to Cocos. And I'm the only one who can give it to you, but you'll have to give me something first. I know you'll do it."

I snorted. Did he know how many men I'd killed?

He folded his arms. "Because if you don't…it would be easy to declare that you're a spy. In peacetime, that might get you imprisoned. But in war…it'll earn you a swift hanging."

Not bloody likely.

"Well, aren't you lovely? Threatening me in my own house, which you've been squatting in. How about you tell me exactly what you want me to do, and then I'll tell you my answer."

The Captain inclined his head. "All right, I'll speak plainly. You join the Australian

Women's Army Service. Do your training, and get sent over to the Command Post on Rottnest. Your job will be to hail every vessel that approaches Fremantle, to find out if they're friend or foe. If they're friendly, send them on, and radio the harbour to expect them. Unfriendly…well, that's what gunners are for. And if you see or hear anything suspicious, you report it to me. Immediately. Until the first ship leaves for Cocos."

Which would be the end of the war. The last one had lasted four years, so why not this one? In 1946, I would be home, and the threat to it would be gone, for the war would be won. One way or another.

I could swim home, but I couldn't protect my girls any more than the rest of my people. To fight a human war, I needed human weapons, and right here, we were sitting on an arsenal. I only hoped it would be enough.

I opened my mouth to agree to his offer.

Triumph flashed in his eyes.

I snapped my mouth shut. "It's not every

day someone tells me to join the army," I said. "I'll need to think about it, and give you my answer in the morning."

I strode away.

"Mrs McGregor, you can't — " Tane began, but the Captain hushed him.

I doubt I was supposed to hear the Captain's words, but the ocean's gift is as much a blessing as it is a curse.

"No harm in waiting until morning. She's got no choice. She knows that, and she'll come around. You'll see."

He was wrong. I did have a choice — to use my knowledge and my skills to help the war effort, or to go home, and use them to guard my family.

Eighteen

I woke to the rumbling of an engine. A motor car, or maybe a truck, judging by the noise. Daylight was already edging around the blockout curtains Tane had made me put up, so I dressed and headed for the kitchen.

Tane was already there, slurping a cup of coffee. "Good morning, Mrs McGregor," he said.

My response wasn't required, as knocking at the front door drew the ensign's attention away from me.

He returned soon after, alone but with a grin on his face. "Have you ever seen an American submarine, Mrs McGregor?"

When I shook my head, he beckoned me toward the veranda. "The first one just arrived. It's a beautiful sight," Tane said.

I headed outside, wanting to judge for myself. I followed his pointing finger to a small submarine with a smashed conning tower, slowly motoring into the harbour in the predawn light.

"It looks like a blue whale tried to mate with it," I remarked. "Is that why it's smaller than the Japanese subs? So it can blend in with whales? The engine's quieter, too − not as powerful."

"The *Sargo* was bombed on the way in. They're lucky the Lockheed Hudson didn't sink it."

Of course. Whales were not the biggest

thing beneath the waves any more. But…"Aren't those your people's planes?"

The Captain last night had talked of a friendly submarine being bombed by trigger happy…oh.

"Yeah, but it's your people in them. It was an Aussie crew bombed one of ours. The Captain's ordered the bomber crew to wait for the submarine to come into port so they could apologise. They've been standing there all night." Tane grinned.

Sure enough, as the sky grew brighter, I could discern a squad of men standing to attention.

"The Quartermaster on the submarine said he wanted to punch the pilot." Tane seemed particularly eager to see this happen, but all I saw was a bunch of handshaking between the submarine crew and their attackers.

I shook my head. Bomb each other to the brink of death, then shake hands and everything was all right. Men and their alliances in times of war. If this was to be the way war went, we'd be lucky if it only took four years.

I could not go home and leave the men to it. I should have brought more sirens with me to help the war effort. But the return trip home and back here would take too much time. Time in which too many men would die.

Had my kind ever allied with humans like this before? Given I was the only one who spoke even one of their languages, I doubted it. So, I would make history.

I bowed my head and took a deep breath, then lifted my eyes to the water, where I'd dived in last night. Swimming home would have to wait.

Then my eyes focussed on something nearer, and I forgot all about water or swimming or anything else.

"What is that?" I breathed, pointing.

Tane followed my gaze and grinned. "That is a Harley Davidson WLA, standard issue army messenger motorcycle. If I get the Captain's permission, I might be able to take you for a short ride around the harbour later."

A ride? Like William would have? Oh, this boy had no idea what sort of woman I was.

I waited until he headed back into the house before I crossed the road to inspect what looked like a lovely replacement for my old Triumph.

I slid into the seat, running my hands down the handlebars as I adjusted to sitting astride something again. This was bigger in every way, and as I kicked the engine into life, I realised this was the very engine that had woken me, or one like it. An engine as powerful as the one in Tony's truck, or at least that's what it sounded like. I opened up the throttle – just a little – and the beast between my legs let out a roar. How could I resist?

Nineteen

When I returned, Tane was pacing up and down the veranda. "What on Earth did you think you were doing?" he demanded, unable to keep the shrill edge of panic out of his voice.

"Going to the WACA," I said, dismounting. I admit I felt a little stiff, for it had been a long time since I'd ridden anything and Tane's

Harley Davidson took more effort to control than my Triumph had, but I tried not to let it show. "Training starts next week. Is the Captain still here?"

Tane was too busy spluttering to reply, so I headed inside.

Captain Green was in the kitchen, drinking coffee.

"I'll do it," I said. "But for a price. I want one of those." I pointed outside.

The Captain choked. "Motorcycles are for soldiers, not women! It's far too heavy for – "

I threw my signup papers on the table. "I took it for a ride out to the WACA. I'm all signed up, and I'll be spying for you before the month is out. But after speaking to some of the other girls signing up with me, I found out that the boarding houses in the city are charging a premium for soldiers to sleep there. And you haven't paid me a penny in rent. Get me one of those Harley things, and you may stay here, rent free, until the end of the war."

Actually, the other girls had said most of

them asked for stockings and cigarettes and other things the US troops had access to that we didn't. I had no need for stockings or cigarettes, but if I was to stay here on land for any length of time, I wanted a new motorcycle. If the Captain refused, I'd buy one myself. And he could stick his spy job up his arse.

"You're giving planes to men who shoot at your submarines. If you want me to carry your messages, I'll need a messenger motorcycle," I said sweetly.

The Captain swallowed the last of his toast. "I will expect weekly reports. You can send them to Tane. If anyone asks, they're love letters."

I couldn't help it. I laughed. "I have a daughter his age, Captain Green. Anyone who knows me won't believe it. I'd be more likely to send love letters to you."

To my delight, the man blushed. "Then send them to Captain Douglas Green," he mumbled into his coffee. He took his time emptying the cup before setting it down and clearing his throat. "And a motorcycle in lieu of rent. I'll speak to the Quartermaster. When do you start training?"

"Next week. Oh, and I told the recruitment officer that you'd sent me, and you wanted me to have the same rank as on my shirt," I said, pulling at the collar. I made no pretence of ignorance this time – I'd learned military ranks and other such things in that American etiquette book on Christmas Island, long ago. "They seemed surprised at first, but I imagine a lieutenant will hear more information than the lower ranks. Of course, aboard the *Islander*, they called me Captain, but it was a civilian vessel, after all."

He stared at me for a moment, before turning his attention to the newspaper on the table.

I took that as my cue to leave.

When I reached my bedroom, I heard him mutter, "I must be a fool for doing this."

"I think it's the right thing," Tane replied.

"Now I know I'm a fool." The Captain

sighed. "And yet…something about her reminds me of Marama."

"Mother?" Tane sounded horrified. "She doesn't look anything like her!"

"But if anyone could swim the length of a harbour, get arrested as a spy, and talk her way into a lieutenant's commission in the army, all in the same day, it's my sister. There's just something about her."

"She stole my motorcycle." Tane sounded petulant.

The Captain laughed. "Now that is something Marama would definitely do. But she wouldn't give it back. Consider yourself lucky I didn't have you up on a charge for it, boy. I've seen better men discharged for less."

Twenty

I must have considered quitting training a thousand times, and each time the sequence was the same. I'd tell the martinet of an officer to shove his commands up his arse, strip off my uniform, then dive nude into the waves at Leighton Beach and swim away.

But once they put a gun in my hands, I changed my mind. The noise and the recoil took some getting used to, and I would never grow accustomed to the stench, but I could hit the target with unerring accuracy.

It was a siren thing, I soon realised, for many of the other women, and a number of men, too, missed more than they hit. Which meant that they needed me to stay and defend Fremantle, for if there weren't enough gunners to take out enemy aircraft and ships, we would lose this port as easily as Keppel Harbour.

We trained on the big guns as well as the small ones, though we weren't allowed to fire the big ones. If it came to battle, that would change, I told myself.

Finally, they lined us uniformed women up on the parade ground, and told us we were going to receive our assignments, for we had completed our training.

I stared longingly at the ocean, wishing I could immerse myself, but I knew it would be some time before I would swim again.

"Lieutenant McGregor!" the training sergeant barked.

Gritting my teeth, I saluted. "Yes, sir!"

"Take your troops to the *Zephyr* and see that they behave themselves. They will be in a camp with men, real soldiers, and I will not have you women distracting them. If you do, you and your troops will be disciplined accordingly by your commanding officer. Do you understand me?"

Oh, I understood him, all right. When the men misbehaved, we would be blamed, because no man could possibly control himself in the presence of a woman. The men on Rottnest Island were about to learn a new lesson in self control, because while I would defend these humans, I had no intention of falling afoul of their failures. "Yes, sir. Perfectly."

The Fremantle Fortress was about to discover that female troops were far superior to anything they'd seen before.

Twenty One

A train waited for us on the jetty when the *Zephyr* berthed, belching kerosene fumes as it chugged all the way up to the parade ground. Luckily, we were led around it into a hall, where a young man in a captain's uniform greeted us.

"I'm Captain Butler, Colonel Thrussell's second in command here on the island, and you will take orders from either him or me, no one else. Under no circumstances will you attempt to give orders to anyone else on this island, unless they are a member of your own unit. I don't care if the rank on your uniform is higher than theirs. The men under my command will obey me, and not you. Do you understand?"

I understood that these men would need a kick up the arse, like most men, before they gave me the respect I deserved. "Yes, sir!" I said, and the other girls joined in.

"You will be rotated through the three different command posts, two weeks to each rotation. You will start here at Bickley, before moving up to Oliver Hill, and then on to Signal Ridge before returning here to the barracks. Your work is of the utmost secrecy, and you are not to gossip about anything you see or hear while you are on the island. Always remember that loose lips sink ships." He pointed emphatically at the poster on the wall.

It was on the tip of my tongue to tell him

that I'd had a hand in sinking more enemy ships than he had, but I doubted Captain Butler would appreciate being out soldiered by a woman. He would keep.

He droned on for a quarter hour longer about all the things we were not allowed to do (not a list any of us would remember), where we would stay (in our own barracks hall, separate from the men) and where we would eat (the mess hall, behind him). Finally, we were allowed to head to the barracks to unpack.

Someone had kindly brought our bags from the train for us, though I admit I would rather have carried them myself than listened to that lecture.

"Lieutenant McGregor!" Captain Butler barked.

It took me a moment to realise he meant me.

I turned and straightened. "Yes, sir?" Inwardly, I cursed my lack of foresight in not insisting the enlistment officers make me a captain instead of a lieutenant. I'd mention it in my first letter to Captain Green.

"As the ranking officer in this barracks hall, I hold you responsible for keeping your troops in line. Or there will be consequences. You're in the military now, and don't think I'll go easy on you because you're women." He attempted to stare me down, failed, then left the room.

Fortunately, he'd departed before several of them broke down into giggles.

"Who died and made him god?" someone said.

More giggles. "The devil, more like."

"Why'd he put her in charge?"

I turned. All eyes were on me, but one pair widened.

"I know you!" she blurted out. "You're Mrs Speranza, from the fish market! When I was little, I wanted to grow up just like you, and boss all the boys around! Even my dad was afraid of you."

Recognition dawned on a few more faces. These girls looked to be in their twenties, so they'd only been children when I left for Christmas Island and William.

"They've torn the fish market down now, and all the fishermen are gone. Where have you been?"

I told them how I'd gone to Christmas Island as William's wife, then glossed over the intervening years until I reached Singapore. They listened, rapt, as I described the burning city, the chaos in the harbour, and our flight to Fremantle.

"No wonder you're a crack shot! I heard you gunned down a submarine that was following you!" one of the girls said.

I winced. Of course someone had spread that story. Then, as now, I chose not to deny it.

"You can definitely handle Captain Butthead, ma'am," the first girl said.

Him, I could handle. Learning their names and taking my place as their leader took a little more effort — at least until breakfast the following morning.

Marion, the girl who'd first recognised me, took her toast with twice as much jam as anyone else I'd ever met. Zolla bemoaned the lack of fish at breakfast, and I had to agree with her. Norma had arms like a professional washerwoman, and I suspected she could punch as hard as any man, though Hilda looked like she could match her for sheer physical strength. Beryl was the tallest, except for me, and Laurel had the sort of figure that could be squeezed into one of the men's uniforms and they'd never know she wasn't one of them. Dolly and Dot took me some time to tell apart, not least because they had similar names, and as we all wore our hair curled into victory rolls and dressed in the same uniforms, until Dolly showed up at breakfast with her hair bundled into a bun, shooting covetous glances at Dot's hair, which, I learned, curled naturally.

There was far more to these women than first appearances, of course – Marion's buried hoard of jam tins at the end of the war has long since passed into legend – and I believe if it weren't for them, I might have swum home and left the humans to fend for themselves.

Fortunately for us all, I did not.

Twenty Two

By the end of the week, there were more than thirty members of the Australian Women's Army Service on the island, divided into three units. The men, who vastly outnumbered us, felt this was a cause for celebration, and persuaded Colonel Thrussell to hold a dance in the main hall at Kingston Barracks to welcome us all.

As the decorations went up and the band tuned their instruments, I was struck with a memory of nights at the Hydrodome with Tony and opened my mouth to remark on it.

"Excuse me, Lieutenant, ma'am," a boy said, lugging a trestle table into the room. He didn't look a day older than Maria, who had been but a baby when I had arrived in Fremantle.

Water, that had been nearly twenty years ago — longer than some of the younger soldiers had been alive. I shook my head. I was old, almost as old as Colonel Thrussell, though I didn't have his grizzled temples yet.

As the sun slowly set, the whole barracks buzzed with excitement. I was one of the few still in uniform, for I'd volunteered to stay on duty while the younger girls had their fun.

"Have you seen the Colonel, Lieutenant?" Captain Butler asked me, peering into the Colonel's office for what had to be the twentieth time.

"No, sir. He's up at West End, I believe." Pegging out the proposed new machine gun installations, a task surely suited to someone of lower rank, but he'd said he was doing it, and I'd not cared to argue. Better than having him here in his office, shouting at me to bring him tea or coffee or whatever else he should have gotten off his arse and grabbed for himself, instead of making me do it.

"He should be back by now, and there's no answer from the radio. It's nearly dark," he said, peering out into the deepening twilight. "Perhaps something has happened."

A coil of dread curled in my gut. Perhaps it had. Surely someone would have radioed, though…unless…

"I could drive you out to West End, so you can see, sir," I said.

Captain Butler stared at me. "You can drive?"

I grinned. "Better than most, sir. When I lived in Fremantle, I used to help Tony drive the fish market truck to make deliveries. My husband and I used to race our motorcycles around Christmas Island. It was quite a challenge, what with the mud and the coconut crabs and all. I have my eye on one of those Harley Davidson messenger motorbikes the Americans ride, and I mean to have one at the end of the war." The one parked outside my house, if I was not mistaken.

"You're not afraid of the rats?" Captain Butler asked.

I almost laughed aloud. I had found Captain Butthead's weakness — quokkas, the local marsupials, which did bear a slight resemblance to giant rats, but only from the back. Quokka faces were not the slightest bit rodent-like — no rat I'd ever seen had such a cheeky smile.

"Captain Butler, have you ever seen a coconut crab? They're three feet wide, with claws big enough to snap your arm. I used to have to chase them out of my garden, where they'd come to hunt the rats that lived under the veranda." I marched toward the nearest jeep, on loan from the Americans who were coming to install the machine guns the Colonel was pegging out. "I'll drive out to West End myself to speak to the Colonel, while you supervise the dance here."

He cast a longing look at the hall. "No, I should go and see what's keeping the Colonel. He might need my help."

There were at least a dozen men stationed at West End, keeping watch for enemy aircraft. What he could do that they couldn't…then again, if no one was answering the radio, maybe something had happened to all of them.

The same thought seemed to have come to Butler, too. "Perhaps I should take a squad of men…"

"I'm the only driver on duty, and the Colonel's orders are for no trucks to be out at night." After some idiots had taken one of the trucks for a joyride and managed to snap the axle in a pothole in the dark. "If we're quick, we could be back before full dark, sir, but only if we take the jeep."

I was on the verge of singing just a little under my breath to get him to agree, when the

Captain suddenly nodded. "Let's go, Lieutenant," he said, climbing into the passenger seat of the jeep.

I was definitely writing to Captain Green to request that promotion in the morning post.

Twenty Three

The sun had already dipped below the horizon, painting the clouds into fluffy pink and gold mangoes, by the time we reached West End. None of the men stationed there had seen the Colonel since lunchtime. They all insisted he'd headed back to the barracks hours ago.

But if he had, we'd have seen him on our way out. And that still didn't explain why no one had responded to the radio.

"We should check the machine gun emplacements, or where they're going to be," I said. I vaguely recalled seeing the map on the Colonel's desk that morning, before he'd rolled it up to take with him. Captain Butler hunched down in his seat, not saying anything. Perhaps he'd seen a quokka.

I drove as near to each of the sites as I could, then walked the rest of the way. There was no sign of the Colonel at any of them.

Finally, I stood on the top of the last clifftop site, and peered out across the water. The moon had found a gap in the clouds, and peeked out to frost the waves and turn the beach sands glowing white. Movement on the beach caught my eye.

Was that a man? I squinted, but couldn't be sure.

I headed down the cliff path to the beach, and with every step, my certainty grew. There were two people standing on the beach, and I thought I could hear faint singing.

It couldn't be.

"Colonel Thrussell, are you all right?" I shouted.

One of the figures started to turn.

The singing grew louder, more insistent, and the turning figure stilled, before striding toward the singer, who could only be another siren.

I bolted down the rest of the path, but I reached the beach too late. Colonel Thrussell and the woman holding his hand were already waist deep in the bay, and then she started to swim, tugging him along after her.

I began to sing, hoping to counteract this strange siren's song, for I did not know her, but the Colonel ducked his head beneath the surface and began to swim, as if my song had no power over him. How was that possible? No siren in the Indian Ocean had a voice more powerful than mine.

Unless she was from somewhere else…

I watched the pair swim out of the cove, where a boat waited to pick them up. No, not a boat…a submarine, sitting on the surface. The pair went below, before the submarine sank out of sight. The unmistakeable rumble of the engines told me all I needed to know.

"Lieutenant McGregor, have you found him?" Captain Butler shouted from the top of the cliff.

Wearily, I trudged back up to tell him what I'd seen. Our mesmerised commanding officer, being kidnapped by a foreign mermaid on a Japanese submarine. Well, I told him she was a woman. No need to mention her tail.

Captain Butler didn't say a word all the way back to the jeep, or on the long drive back to the barracks. The dance was well underway by the time we reached the main hall, but neither of us felt like joining the festivities, so we skirted the revellers and headed to our separate barracks.

Twenty Four

The Colonel didn't reappear, and the next day brought detectives from the mainland to investigate. They headed out to West End with Captain Butler, before interrogating every man who'd seen the Colonel before his disappearance.

Stuck at the secretary's desk outside the Colonel's office, which the detectives had claimed for themselves, I waited for my turn. I waited all day…but they never called me in.

When they left on the *Zephyr* that evening, they took Captain Butler with them.

It wasn't until I headed to the mess hall for dinner that night that I heard the whispers. Not only had Colonel Thrussell disappeared without a trace, but all the maps and plans of Fremantle Fortress, too, including the new machine gun emplacements. The Americans were loud in their displeasure, for they'd planned to start work on the gun turrets today, and the detectives hadn't let them near any of the sites.

Three days later, an urgent radio communication came from West End: a body had washed up on the beach.

They brought it to the hospital, to wait for the detectives to come from the mainland. The men paid me no attention as I slipped into the room and twitched the sheet away from the sodden corpse.

It was Colonel Thrussell, all right. I could

see enough of his face to be sure, even with the bullet holes in his head.

When the detectives came, they shook their heads and said the cause of death was suicide.

But I knew the truth.

Twenty Five

The Americans had heard some version of the true story, too, I found, for they built double the number of gun emplacements than had been originally planned. One set where the original plans said they'd be, and a second set overlooking the shipping channels, on the cliffs closer to the settlement. Only the second set actually got guns – the places that had been on Colonel Thrussell's map got pieces of wood painted to look like guns, and the one on the hill behind Kingston Barracks even got its own fake railway, too.

The real railway had fish names, including the two locomotives, Crab and Crayfish, but the fake rail line soon earned the impressive moniker of the Orient Express.

None of the men would tell me why, but the girls were far more forthcoming.

"It's because things go very fast up there," Marion said, blushing furiously.

Dot gave her a push. "Only if you go there with men," she said.

Marion's face blazed. "Only one man. Not like Eileen from the other unit. She has ever so many nylons, now she spends her nights up there with the American soldiers…"

They both looked anxiously at me. I vaguely remembered Captain Butler saying something about good behaviour and how anything else would be my fault.

Well, if it was good enough for the male

soldiers, it was certainly good enough for my girls. Besides, Captain Butler had not returned, and we had a new commanding officer, a Colonel Williams. I admit I preferred him to his predecessor, for the first thing Colonel Williams did when he arrived was to promote me to captain, with the new patch sent over from Captain Green.

The second thing he did was send my unit up to Signal Ridge, beneath the lighthouse in the middle of the island, where we were expected to code messages and orders and such, like we'd trained for.

We shared a house up there, an old lighthouse keeper's cottage, which we had orders to lock up tight at night, so that the men camped out in their tents in the valley below could not get in.

Of course, that didn't stop them from trying.

Twenty Six

The most persistent of the soldiers was a particularly nasty piece of work by the name of Gunner Heeren. He came to the door of the house, several times a day, demanding to be allowed in. When asked why, he always said that one of the girls had invited him to visit.

Every time, I would go and ask the girls who were home if they'd invited the bounder.

Everyone shook their heads, and I'd shoo him away again.

Finally, when we'd gone two days without hearing his knock at the door, I dared to believe he'd given up.

But we were not so lucky.

The back door slammed, and Zolla came running into the kitchen, her face paler than the margarine the mess hall was now using, with butter being rationed.

"He's out there," she gasped out, clutching her shirt. Only then did I see several of the buttons had been ripped off.

"Who?" I asked, though I already knew.

"Gunner Heeren. He tried to grab me, but I kicked him in the shins and wrenched away. He's still out there, waiting by the outhouse…" She peered out through the back windows.

I leaned over her shoulder to do the same. Sure enough, I could see a dark shadow in the bushes beside the dunny.

I felt an urgent desire to use the facilities. "Lock the door behind me," I instructed her.

"Don't unlock it unless it's me."

Zolla nodded, her lips pressed too tightly together to let any words out.

I marched up to the outhouse.

"Have you come back to me? You know you want it," Heeren said.

"The only thing I want is to sit my arse on that toilet seat and rid my body of the travesty the mess hall called mashed potatoes last night," I said archly. "I knew there was something wrong with it when the first mouthful was crunchy. Now, get out of my way, and leave my girls alone."

"I'm not interested in you, you old trout," the Gunner spat.

I didn't look a day older than the girls under my command, and I knew it. "That's Captain Trout, ma'am, or I'll see you get reassigned to KP for long enough to learn how to make mashed potatoes properly."

"You're not a real officer, and I don't have to listen to you. I don't take orders from no woman. Not now, not ever!" he shouted as he marched off into the darkness.

I considered letting him go. After all, the recruiters on the radio kept saying we needed every able bodied man to defend the country, and I certainly fancied that he'd make good cannon fodder, but the Japanese weren't using cannons. They were using guns, and planes, and submarines, and sirens they'd brought from the Pacific Ocean, killing innocent people like the civilians in Singapore, instead of bullying snot rags like Gunner Heeren.

And one day, when the war was over, he'd still be preying on women, demanding things he did not deserve, unless I put a stop to it.

So I strode off into the darkness, too, my night vision so much better than his. When I approached the lookout post where he was supposed to be standing watch, I found him smoking a cigarette with his back to the water, the burning red end guiding me to him as surely as a drop of blood's drew a shark.

He never saw me grab his gun, nor the blow that dropped him to his knees. I hefted the gun onto my hip and set the barrel to the back of his head. This was a Bren machine gun, and not one of the lighter rifles we'd practiced with on the shooting range. At point blank range, though, I didn't doubt I'd be accurate.

"I want to hear you say you'll never touch a woman without her permission again," I said.

"Sod off!"

I hit him over the head with the barrel, then set it against the back of his head as I began to hum a song of control. When I felt him sag, I knew the song had taken hold. "Say the words."

"I said sod off, you withered old trout! I'm not taking orders from – "

The gun went off in my hands, sounding like a thousand men hammering on the cottage door.

Heeren dropped to the ground.

If a thousand men hammered on the cottage door, he would never again be one of them. He'd need a head for that, and most of his was missing.

A human might have felt guilty. But I was a siren, and Heeren deserved to be fed to the sharks.

So I dropped the gun and headed back home.

Later that night, I alone lay awake in the bunkroom we all shared. My girls were asleep, their beds all lined up in the lighthouse beam that lit the room for less than a second before the five seconds of darkness that was the Rottnest Island Light Station's signature. Safe.

Just as safe as I hoped my daughters were, in their underwater beds, on the other side of the Indian Ocean. I longed for the war to end, so that we all might go home and be reunited with our families again.

When morning dawned, the Command Post was full of whispers. Someone had found what remained of Gunner Heeren. It must have been suicide, Colonel Williams said.

Though I did not regret my actions, I hoped Heeren's death would be the last.

Twenty Seven

Colonel Williams was a stickler for training exercises, insisting we must be ready when the time came. Unlike his predecessor, he included us women in his training schedule, and I came to enjoy the sessions on the shooting range. Oh, the rifles were noisy and smelly, and my shoulder hurt for hours afterward, but seeing the girls improve as the weeks went on was a matter of considerable pride. The men, not to be outdone, redoubled their efforts until even Colonel Williams felt the need to praise them for it.

Their reward came in the form of, you guessed it, another training exercise, with some of the short range coastal defences. The Colonel wanted them to practice their marksmanship with the six inch guns at Bickley Battery. The target was a barge towed behind a boat. It floated so low in the water, I'd have been surprised if they could hit it with a rifle, let alone the big six inch guns.

In fact, the men on the boat soon found just how bad their comrades' aim was, as a stream of swearing came out of the radio, telling them to hit the barge and not the boat.

"You're shooting like girls — one hand over your eyes like you're afraid to hit something, and firing wildly in all directions!" one of the engineers taunted, sitting up on the ridge to watch the show.

Us girls were perched on the ridge, too,

waiting our turn. We'd had the same training as the men, so we could fire these guns if the need arose, but it looked like the men needed the practice more than we did.

The next shot went wide, carving a chunk of rock off an island a couple hundred yards behind the barge.

At this rate, they'd run out of ammunition and flatten Phillip Rock to the waterline before hitting the barge.

"Still shooting like a girl!"

My patience ran out and I jumped to my feet. "If a girl was shooting, we'd have sunk the barge by now!"

The men laughed, Colonel Williams with them, until the Colonel held up his hand for silence. "Let the AWAS have a shot. Captain McGregor?"

"Yes, sir." I glanced at the windsock, noting the speed and direction of the breeze that had blown up since they'd started shooting.

I smoothed my skirt and made my way down the hill to the gun emplacement, with my unit following behind me like obedient ducklings. If anything, the jeering only grew louder.

Up close, the six inch gun was bigger than I'd expected. Oh, the barrel was six inches wide, of course, but it was more than six yards long. No wonder it took a crew of nine men to load and fire it. I hoped my girls would have the strength to move it into position, as well as load it.

If not, at least there were plenty of useless men around who could lend a hand.

"Load," I said softly.

Norma and Beryl gritted their teeth, struggling under the weight of the shell, but they brought it over to the barrel and loaded it into the breech. Zolla wielded the rammer, before moving aside to let Marion load the charge.

I squinted at the barge for a long moment, judging the distance and the heading, then factored in the breeze. Only then did I give the girls the command to shift the gun into position.

"She didn't call for a bearing!" one of the men jeered, amid much laughter.

I hid my smile. What these men did not know what that every firing command they received from the Command Post came from one of us. When you spend all day, peering through spyglasses, calculating angles and relaying them to the necessary defence posts, it became second nature. Besides, if we were to radio the Command Post for instructions, none would be forthcoming, because we were all here.

Colonel Williams knew what his men did not, so while they laughed and jeered, he stood silent.

Dot and Dolly worked one wheel, while Hilda and Laurel took charge of the other one. When they were done, I sighted along the barrel, then nodded my approval.

I opened my mouth to give the command to fire, then thought the better of it. I was the best shot out of all of us, so I should be the one to fire the gun. When the shell hit, we'd share the victory. I wrapped my fingers around the lanyard.

"Fire," I said, yanking hard.

A collective gasp rose up from the girls, and we all held our breath, counting the seconds as the shell rose up, before arcing down again, speeding toward its target – a spot between the boat and the barge. We didn't hear it hit, but I imagine the shell made little sound as it dived into the water, shearing through the rope that held the barge to the boat towing it.

The result was immediate – a fountain of swearing erupted from the radio, as a wave swamped the barge and it began to sink.

Except for the crackling and swearing from the radio, silence swept over the watching men. Then out of it rose a slow clap – Colonel Williams, applauding us.

I saluted. "Target eliminated, sir."

The Colonel nodded. "Well done, AWAS. Dismissed."

I led my unit back to the barracks, for a

well-earned afternoon off.

The men spent the rest of the afternoon trying to save the barge, then tie it back up to the boat, before learning how to shoot as well as the girls who'd bested them.

I bet that never made it into the history books.

Twenty Eight

Colonel Williams called me into his office.

"Yes, sir?" I asked. I hoped whatever he wanted, it wouldn't take long. The mess hall had been promising roast beef for Sunday dinner for a week now, and I didn't mean to miss out.

"You haven't taken any leave. You've been stationed here for half a year, and not once have you left the island."

I'd certainly been tempted. Sometimes, I missed Apalala so much, I almost dived into the water and started to swim back to Cocos, submarines and ships be damned. Other nights, when the supply ship was delayed and all the mess hall had was overcooked vegetables turned into tasteless mush, I came so close to going for a swim to catch a few fish so that I could have a decent meal. But that wasn't what the Colonel was talking about.

I'd seen the other girls board the *Zephyr* and head back to the mainland to visit their families. Marion had met her beau, Alan, on the *Zephyr* during such a trip, a story she told every time the girls shared a bottle of sherry.

"I didn't know I needed to, sir," I said honestly.

He made a displeased grumbling sound in his throat. "Everyone has to take a week's leave. It's the law."

Not a law I'd heard about, so it must have been something the West Australian government did in the last ten years, for we'd never had anything like paid holidays in the fish market. We'd taken days off for bad weather and Christmas and Easter, when the markets were closed, but that was it. "If you say so, sir."

He slapped his hand down on the desk. "Indeed I do. Pack your things. You're headed back to Fremantle on the *Zephyr* tonight."

No roast beef for me, then. "Yes, sir," I said, and headed to the barracks.

Twenty Nine

In the months since I'd been gone, Aunt Merry's house had changed again. A boxy brick structure stood beside the house, and fresh boards had been laid across the veranda.

I found Captain Green in the kitchen, sipping coffee as he read the morning newspaper. There was no sign of Tane.

"Good morning," I said. "Is the kettle still

hot?" Might as well make myself some tea, if we had any. Rationing meant there wasn't always tea on the menu in the mess hall, but there'd been plenty here when I left, and Captain Green and Tane didn't drink it, so, if I was lucky…I gave a squeak of triumph as I found Merry's tea tin still brimming with leaves. It wasn't my Japanese green tea, but with the war on, I'd take whatever I could get. I began to brew a pot.

Captain Green set down his newspaper. "I'm surprised to see you so soon."

I laughed. "It's been six months, Captain. I know we've both been busy with the war and all, but that's hardly what I'd consider soon."

"No, it's that I only asked Williams yesterday when you'd have shore leave."

Now I understood. "And Colonel Williams took that as a hint to send me on the next boat home."

"Quite obliging of him, really. I'll have to send him over a carton of cigarettes to thank him."

"I think he'd prefer whiskey, actually. I've never seen Colonel Williams smoke."

Green gave me a calculating look. "Whiskey it is, then, though that may be harder to find. Worth it, though, to keep him onside, as he's our first line of defence. Heaven knows why they put a man like Thrussell in charge, when I think of him turning traitor…"

Captain Green had, of course, received my full report about Thrussell's disappearance and death, though I had left off mentioning that the woman was a siren.

"Some men do the strangest things when there's a woman involved, sir," I said carefully. I might not have liked Thrussell, but he'd been under the siren's control when he deserted his post, and he hadn't deserved to die.

He waved his hand airily. "Leave off the sirs and ranks and things here. I have your reports. What I want is for you to speak frankly. I needed to see you face to face, for some things cannot be trusted to a letter."

He looked so serious, I knew the news

could not be good.

"Indeed they cannot," I prompted.

Green sighed. "There have been sighting of Japanese ships and submarines up and down the coast. Never close enough to engage, but enough to have everyone on high alert. Have you heard or seen any of them, out at Rottnest?"

Slowly, I shook my head. "Not since the one that took Colonel Thrussell." That didn't mean they weren't out there, though. I hadn't been in the water since my failed attempt to swim out of Fremantle Harbour. Sound travelled further beneath the waves, and I'd hear the unmistakeable rumble of a Japanese submarine from miles away if I was in the water with it. Maybe I should patrol the waters at night. As long as no one saw me…

Green nodded. "Keep an ear and an eye out. I want to hear if you do. There are rumours of a planned attack on Fremantle, establishing a beach head from which to take the rest of the country. No word on when or how, which has the High Command mighty uncomfortable. Half of them expect another attack like Pearl Harbor, while the others think it's something more stealthy. There were Japanese pearlers up in Broome, who know the waters up that way all too well, so we've confiscated as many boats as we could, and burned the rest, so they won't try that."

"Where are the luggers now?" I asked.

"Safe."

I shook my head. "You can't just commandeer boats like that, and expect people to accept it. Fishing is an important food source, and income, for a lot of families along the coast. Even if it's not safe for them to go out fishing now, those boats need to be maintained, because they'll want them back after the war. Captain, you're a naval man yourself – surely you understand that if you threaten to destroy their boats, the men who sail in them will fight to their last breath to defend them."

"I'm not a complete fool, Mrs McGregor. I

sent the boats to the Houtman Abrolhos, on a training exercise."

I drew in a sharp breath. "I bet that was an unmitigated disaster. How many of them remain?"

"You're right about it being a disaster. We didn't lose any, but only because we hired fishermen from Geraldton to sail them. Even then, our soldiers were stranded on one of the islands for several days before conditions were calm enough to get them off the island safely."

I shook my head. "You should have pulled me off signal duty. I could have captained one of those boats, or at least made sure your soldiers weren't stranded."

Green laughed. "I bet you could, but the High Command could barely stomach letting fishermen with Italian ancestors out on those boats. If I'd suggested putting a woman in charge…they'd think I'd gone mad. Besides, if what I hear from Colonel Williams is true, we need you manning the guns out at Rottnest. So far, you're the only gunner at Bickley to have actually managed to sink your target."

To the mortification of all of Colonel Williams' men. It wasn't my fault they'd been given guns that were old before the First World War, or that they didn't have a siren's instinctive grasp of the physics of motion in water and air.

"What do you want, Captain?" I asked tiredly.

"I want to know where you think they will attack. You've seen the Japanese in action at Christmas Island and Cocos, in Singapore and at sea. If they're coming for us…I want to know what your gut says." He unrolled a map on the table, using his coffee cup and plate to hold the corners down. "You've sailed this coastline, and you know it as well as anyone. Where will they strike first, and how do we stop them?"

I studied the map of the West Australian coastline. Most of it was empty, with a few small, scattered towns. Much like Pulu Keeling, if they wanted to build a secret fuel store, or a base from which to attack, they could come ashore anywhere, and no one would know until it was too late. But… "They could pick anywhere, any place where there's a beach and no one around. But the best place to pick would be somewhere near deep water, so the submarines could get in real close before having to surface, and the warships, too. Water where seaplanes could land. If I wanted to conquer Fremantle, I'd first have to take Rottnest."

He brought another map out, this time one that showed Rottnest Island, with all the little rocks and islets and reefs around it. "Where will they come ashore?"

I shrugged. "They could come ashore anywhere. West End's where the deepest water is, which is why the submarine could get so close, but they'd also have to walk all the way up to Signal Ridge and Oliver Hill, so it's not a very good invasion point. If they really want to take Rottnest, they'd have to come ashore here, at Bickley." I pointed to the beach below the barracks, well within range of all our six inch guns, not to mention some of the machine gun nests. "They'd need to come at night, quick and quiet, likely in small craft that no one would see until they reached the beach, and then it would be too late. They'd need to take out all the Bickley defences, and gain control of the barracks at the same time. Then they could take the train up to Oliver Hill and Signal Ridge. Without any warning, they'd be sitting ducks…"

I waited for him to argue, but found him nodding instead.

Green tapped the Natural Jetty, a rocky bar at the end of the beach. "I think we should conduct another training exercise. Let's call it Operation Dhufish…"

Thirty

When Colonel Williams sent my unit down to dinner early, I knew something was up, especially when men I didn't know took our places in the Command Post.

Nothing out of the ordinary happened during dinner, though, so when the girls went back to our barracks, I lingered by the mess hall. One of the gunners who'd been assigned to the kitchen had been training as a chef before he joined up, and he'd made the most delightful seasoning for the fish. Though I tended to eat my fish raw, if I stayed on land long enough, I might find the time to put his recipe into practice.

"The secret's in the salt. You pack rosemary sprigs into it, and just leave it for a week or two. Then you have to make sure it's ground up real fine…"

Shouts came from the beach, followed by the boom of one of the guns, then another. When no alarm sounded to call us to arms, my suspicions were confirmed.

Captain Green's Dhufish had landed.

"What's happening?" Gunner Fry asked, his eyes wide with what might have been fear.

"I think we're under attack," I said slowly. It wasn't until a bunch of dusty, black-clad men came charging up the track from the beach that I was certain. Our gunners had actually managed to hit their targets — albeit with flour bombs, but it was a start.

"Get back! I'll protect you, Captain!" Gunner Fry shouted, racing toward the men.

"No, wait – " I began, but he let rip with a stream of invective that drowned out anything I might have said.

He had two of them down on the ground before I could blink, and he was off, chasing several more back the way they had come.

By the time I caught up, he'd managed to corner two of them in an evacuation trench, halfway to the beach. Both had blooming black eyes and from the way one of them was favouring his left side, I suspected he had some broken ribs to go with it.

"Gunner Fry, I command you to stop!" I shouted.

"But, Captain…"

I pointed at the one whose ribs hadn't been broken yet. "Which unit are you from, soldier?"

He grimaced. Maybe he was more injured than I thought. "Z Special, ma'am."

I slid down into the trench, angling my body

between Fry and his prisoners. "Stand down, Gunner. That's an order. They're on our side, and this is just a training exercise. Operation Dhufish."

"Yes, ma'am." Gunner Fry reluctantly backed off.

I turned to the injured men and held out a hand to help the nearest one up. "Did you come here in the luggers, or did Captain Green find you something less conspicuous?"

He winced as he rose to his feet, then managed a grin. "Three luggers and an old Malayan fishing boat. I don't know where the Captain got it, but…it's perfect."

I sent Gunner Fry and one of the other kitchenhands to help the men to the hospital, hoping they'd be patched up and whole again in time to rejoin their unit on that deceptively derelict fishing boat. They'd be remembered as heroes if they managed to complete the mission Green and I had come up with over the breakfast table.

Thirty One

"Oh, move over! You don't need to spend as much time primping as the rest of us – Alan would happily dance with you all night if you wore nothing but a flour sack!"

"By the way Alan looks at her, he'd be happier still if she forgot the flour sack."

"You're all just jealous!" Marion declared, but there was no hiding the smile on her face as she graciously made space for the other girls in front of the washroom mirror.

I stayed out of their way. While I did intend to go to the dance with them, I knew that they'd all have partners for every dance even if they all wore flour sacks, because the men outnumbered us more than ten to one. So I donned a dress – bought on my last week of leave over on the mainland, as what clothes I had were either uniforms or hopelessly outdated. The dresses I'd worn to dance halls twenty years ago would only draw unwanted attention. Not to mention questions about my age.

An ear-splitting screech sliced through the chatter.

"Who's killing a cat?" Norma snapped, looking ready to strangle whoever was tormenting poor puss.

"No one, silly! It's the air raid siren!"

"But who'd be flying over here, now?"

"The Japanese, or course! We're at war!"

"No, they can't be. It must be another drill."

All eyes turned to me. I was their commanding officer, after all.

"Drill or not, we're supposed to go hide in the trenches if we're not on duty when the siren sounds," I reminded them.

"But I haven't finished doing my hair!" Dolly wailed.

I shrugged. "So take the curlers and pins with you. Who knows how long we'll be waiting in the trenches? It could be hours."

Hilda sniffed. "It's not like they'll call on us to man the guns."

It might come to that, if enough men were killed, but I didn't voice what we were all thinking. Instead, I grabbed a bag and held it open. "Here, put all your things in here. I'll carry it down to the trenches, and you can finish up down there."

A short moment later, I threw the bulging bag over my shoulder as I followed the girls at a run for the trenches we were assigned to shelter in.

Illuminated by a single lantern and a couple

of cigarette lighters, the girls took turns holding the compact mirrors for each other as they finished their preparations.

When the faint roaring began to grow louder, I looked up. A Japanese float plane – was that an Emily? – soared overhead, climbing as it headed west. Either we weren't its target, or it was coming around for a better angle of approach to bomb us.

A hush fell over the trenches, as we all held our collective breaths, wishing it would go away and that no more planes would follow. At least, that's what I wished for. It seemed more sensible than wishing our gunners would shoot it down, seeing as it was rapidly heading out of range, if it wasn't already.

When they sounded the all clear and we were allowed to leave the trenches, the girls were all ready for the dance.

While that one plane might have reminded us we were still at war, it also reminded us we were still alive. And while life might be fleeting, we should dance while we still could.

That night, even I didn't sit down for more than five minutes, for at some point in the trenches, I'd caught the girls' fever for fun.

It wasn't until the next morning that the real implications of that plane sank in.

Thirty Two

Daily, we were urged to be more vigilant on our watches, radioing in every ship, submarine and aircraft the moment we spotted or heard it, as if we hadn't been doing that already. Security checks were more stringent, and some nights I couldn't even slip unseen down to the beach for a swim.

When I couldn't patrol the water, I

volunteered for the night watches, for my night vision was far superior to any human's. It wasn't tested until one night a ship came steaming in, refusing all hails and definitely not giving the correct codes.

Panic ensued. Suddenly all the guns needed to be pointed at it, while the other ships were warned away.

I'd already calculated the bearings they needed, and someone else was painstakingly sending those through to the guns. In the lull while I waited for orders, I grabbed a pair of binoculars and raced outside for a better look.

Sure enough, the speeding ship was visible, but the outline was familiar. "It's a Liberty Ship, and if they continue on their present course, they'll hit a reef!" I called.

Colonel Williams came to take the binoculars out of my hands so that he could see for himself. "Are you sure?"

"Yes! Fire a warning shot, sir, or we'll be overrun with Americans in the morning, all complaining about us sinking their ship, when it's their sailors who are being reckless about the reefs."

Thrussell would have ignored me, but Colonel Williams was a very different man.

Tension crackled through the Command Post, with a dangerous current of disapproval beneath it. I was the only woman on duty that night, and though I outranked most of them, they still didn't like taking orders from me. They itched to hear the Colonel reprimand me instead of doing the sensible thing and following my orders.

Men were so easy to control. No song needed tonight.

I grinned. "It's a Liberty Ship. I'd bet my brassiere on it, sir."

Every set of eyes went to my chest.

Less than a minute later, a warning shot flew across the ship's bow, followed by a terse radio command to halt, identify themselves and give the correct security codes, or we'd open fire.

Out on the water, the ship ground to a halt, none too soon. Their bow wave broke on the reef with a foam of white water.

"Don't shoot, don't shoot — what the bloody hell is that? Why is there a rock there in the water? We're the *Winslow Homer*. Now who has the blasted code books?" crackled the response.

Everyone in the room relaxed as one, and laughter rang out from one man, before he was hushed.

It took half an hour for the ship's crew to find their security codes, after which the Colonel ordered them to change course so they'd miss the reef and steam safely into Fremantle Harbour.

The next morning, when I checked the roster, I found that the Colonel had removed my name from the night watches. I considered protesting, but it wasn't my job to save all the ships from their sailors' stupidity, so I decided to spend my nights swimming instead.

Thirty Three

Rumours reached us of a huge Japanese fleet, massing in Keppel Harbour, for the sole purpose of attacking Australia and claiming it as their own. Their target? Fremantle, of course, which now held more US ships and submarines than Pearl Harbor at its peak, not to mention Australian, Dutch and British ships that were also crowding our harbour.

At first, we didn't want to believe them, until the coded messages started to come in from Cocos, confirming not only the fleet's existence, but that it was big enough to do serious damage if it ever reached Fremantle.

Someone in the fleet must have intercepted one of those messages, for the next thing we heard, Cocos was under attack from the air — Japanese planes bombed Home Island, and it was civilians who suffered. I hoped my daughters had been far away, deep beneath the surface when the planes flew over, but I would not know for sure until I could return there to see for myself.

High Command gave the order to evacuate Fremantle Harbour, sending every ship and submarine south to Princess Royal Harbour, at Albany. Fear stalked the streets of Fremantle, for the city seemed undefended, with the port so empty. Never mind that Fremantle Fortress was fully manned, with guns pointed in all directions — if the fall of Singapore had taught us anything, it would not be enough. The troops who had taken Singapore hadn't cared if they killed soldiers or civilians, and Fremantle would be no different.

Someone had to stop the fleet, before it reached Fremantle, but no one knew where it was. They sailed under radio silence, and they could be anywhere between Cocos and here.

The Colonel ordered us to scramble all our codes, and send out coded nonsense messages all day and night. Everyone – including us women – were expected to sleep in our uniforms, so that we'd be ready at a moment's notice if the fleet attacked. The whole of Fremantle Fortress was on red alert, and still it would not be enough.

And then…what Merry would have called a miracle happened, though it did not seem so at the time. A coded distress call came in from a merchant ship, north of the Houtman Abrolhos. The *Behar* was under attack…before the radio fell eerily silent.

As luck would have it, I was the one tasked with translating the message…and when I had,

I took it straight to Colonel Williams. Though most of the troops were not aware of the fleet that had left Singapore, the Colonel hadn't managed to keep the news from me. The High Command needed to know about the *Behar* immediately, but with the nonsense codes we were broadcasting, we couldn't risk sending word by radio.

Which is how I ended up as the sole passenger aboard the *Zephyr*, steaming at full speed for Fremantle.

I went straight to Captain Green, knowing he was my most direct channel to the High Command, and told him everything I knew about the *Behar*, along with what I suspected. Then I went home and made a cup of tea.

Thirty Four

By the time Captain Green arrived back at my house, I was drinking my third pot of tea out on the veranda, waiting for him.

He trudged up the steps and slumped into the seat across from me. I poured him a cup of tea. He was so drained, he drank it without even looking at it.

"What do we have up north that can stop

this fleet?" I asked.

Green shook his head. "Nothing."

"What about the Allied troops at Ceylon?" I pressed.

"They've been ordered to stay close to home and not engage unless they're attacked."

The British High Command were cowards. I'd known that in Singapore, but I knew it even more so now. The only territory they protected was England. If the rest of us were tortured to death or blown to bits, they wouldn't care, as long as they could keep their own miserable island.

We were on our own, and it would not be enough.

Unless…

If one of their warships were to turn on the others, that would stop them. Well, until the traitorous ship sank. Then if they still didn't turn back, another ship would have to turn traitor, until they were all destroyed, or everyone aboard them was dead.

Of course, convincing an entire ship to

attack its allies was no easy task.

Well, unless you were a siren who'd done it before…

"Send me up there," I said.

I could swim it, but I wouldn't be there in time.

"Put me on one of the flying boats, and fly me up to Potshot," I said. It was the American nickname for the secret military base at Exmouth — so secret, the Japanese had bombed it twice the week it opened. "I'll be your eyes, the advance warning you need."

Captain Green almost dropped his cup. "I can't send a woman into combat! The High Command would have my hide."

"Reconnaissance, not combat," I argued. "Besides, if we don't stop that fleet before it reaches Fremantle, combat will come here, and I'd like to meet the man willing to tell me I can't fight when those bloody Zeroes are coming here to bomb my house. I'll get my hands on one of those Bren machine guns and shoot them out of the sky."

The Captain looked mighty uncomfortable. Maybe because he knew there was an arsenal of weapons in the cellar under the garage he'd built beside my house, and he didn't want to admit it to me. Or maybe because he knew Gunner Heeren had met the wrong end of a Bren, and he suspected I knew more about it than I'd told him.

"Put me on a flying boat, Douglas," I said slowly. "You need me in the north-west, not here. I'll fly up there, see what there is to see, and come right back to tell you all about it. I won't shoot anybody, I promise."

He managed a weak smile. "If I had anyone else to send, I would. If anyone finds out…"

"No one but you and I will ever know," I promised him.

After all, no one keeps secrets quite as well as a siren.

Thirty Five

So much for a secret base. Potshot was little more than a few dusty runways and a bunch of dust-covered fuel tanks. I wasn't sure if that was supposed to be camouflage, or if the dust was so ubiquitous, the tanks were impossible to keep clean. I considered asking the cows, which were more numerous than the human population, but they were as close-mouthed as the men. I put that down to my appearance.

Captain Green had found me a men's uniform to wear over one of my old flapper corsets. With some artfully placed padding and my hair pinned painfully under my cap, I looked like a paunchy middle-aged officer who'd seen more good dinners than combat. When I started asking questions about a merchant vessel no one else had heard of, with everyone's focus on the approaching fleet, my place as a pariah was confirmed.

They left me alone, which was exactly what I wanted, because when night fell, I headed out into the open ocean. Past Ningaloo Reef with its miles of hard coral, reminding me of The Gap at Cocos, and off the continental shelf into deep water.

The dolphins answered my call, and, like the gossips they were, they were only too happy to tell me where the *Behar* had sunk in a battle scant days ago.

I swam until I heard the throbbing engines of a Japanese submarine, a sound I followed to its source.

The fleet spanned fifty miles of ocean, spread out to make it more difficult to attack, I imagined…or for one ship to turn on the others and do much damage. I swore and headed in closer to the nearest warship, a heavy cruiser called the *Tone*. An apt name for a vessel I was about to sing into submission, I thought.

I debated whether to climb aboard the ship, but I decided there was no need. I'd controlled the crews of the *Sydney* and the *Emden* thirty years ago from beneath the surface, and now I was older and wiser, I could easily do the same now. I swam along the hull, listening to the voices of the crew inside. One spot seemed to be noisier than the rest. The galley, maybe? The more people I could reach, the better.

I took a deep breath and began to weave a song of control. Softly, at first, until the hull began to resonate with my song, amplifying it to those inside.

"What's that singing?" I clearly heard

someone say. In English, not in Japanese.

"It sounds like a woman."

"Don't be daft, why would there be a woman on a warship?"

Someone began hammering on the bulkhead inside.

"Hey, we're the crew of the *Behar*. Civilians. They took us prisoner, and now they're holding us in this hot store room with no food or water. They're trying to kill us!"

For the first time in my life, I stammered to a stop. I'd seen enough innocent civilians killed in this war. The citizens of Singapore. Whoever had died during the bombing of Home Island. The stories of all the refugees who'd found their way home to Fremantle after Singapore fell. I couldn't let the warships attack one another, if it meant more civilians would die. That would make me no better than the people I was fighting.

The humans who would attack Fremantle unless I disbanded this fleet.

I couldn't send it to the bottom of the sea

with civilians on board.

But I might be able to convince them to go back to where they'd come from…

Thirty Six

Fifty miles I had to swim, or at least that's what it felt like, up and down the length of the convoy. Sending the hulls of ships and submarines reverberating with my song, until everyone in the fleet believed they'd been ordered to head back, because the Allied forces along the West Australian coast were prepared for them, and if they continued, they'd all be lost.

If they ignored my orders and continued along their current path, I'd be forced to choose between the lives of the *Behar*'s crew and the people in Fremantle – a choice I didn't want to make. So I sang on, thankful for the warm salt water coating my throat that kept me from going hoarse. I sang until the ships really did change course, and head for Singapore.

Only then did I turn toward the shore.

I knew I should head back to Potshot, to catch a flight back to Perth, but even the thought of having to stab myself with all those pins, while wearing all that stifling padding, made me want to go in another direction entirely – to Cocos, where my daughters were surely waiting for me, wondering why I'd been gone so long.

But when it came down to it, I'd sworn an oath to serve in the Australian Women's Army Service as long as I was needed, and I knew Captain Green deserved to know Fremantle was safe from the invasion fleet. There was no more capable messenger than me, for I'd seen the fleet's retreat with my own eyes.

So I enjoyed my swim, lingering a little on the reef to snack on an emperor or two, before heading ashore in the darkness to the red dirt air strip, and my flight to Fremantle.

Thirty Seven

On my return, I was told I could not return to Rottnest, lest people ask too many questions about my absence. My only regret was that I hadn't had time to say farewell to the girls in my unit, for I never did see them again. Or if I did, they were much older and no longer recognisable as the girls I once knew.

Captain Green arranged for me to be reassigned to the secret silo signal station atop one of the wheat silos in North Fremantle. Ever day, I climbed up the two hundred and eleven steps through a swirling cyclone of wheat chaff, wondering if this was the day I'd choke on it, but I never did. I decoded the signals we received, then encoded replies and sent them out into the airwaves, for with the invasion fleet no longer on the way, it was considered safe to send messages without nonsense in them.

Not that that stopped some of the orders coming through – men could be such idiots sometimes – but the consequences were becoming less dire, at least for the Allies. It began to look like the war really would end.

The men in the signal station began asking if I was looking forward to the end of the war, when I might be allowed to be a normal housewife with children again. I didn't have the heart to tell them that I never was, and never would be a housewife, but I did admit I longed to see my children again.

At the end of my shift, I'd head down those

stairs, hop on the Harley Davidson Captain Green had provided, and let the sea breeze we called the Fremantle Doctor blow the chaff off my clothes on the way home.

Then I would join Captain Green in the Officers' Mess for dinner, which I probably wasn't supposed to do, but none of the men dared to take it up with Captain Green. I suspect they thought I was his lover, as well as his landlady, and perhaps if we had met in another time, I might have been.

Germany surrendered, but Japan doggedly fought on, so I kept on going to the silo, waiting for the signal that said Japan had surrendered, too.

Word came of the nuclear bombs dropped on Japan, so many civilians dead, and I wondered if the cost was worth it. Still they did not surrender.

I came home to find Lucy standing on my veranda, the excitement shimmering in her eyes making her look ten years younger. It had to be good news.

"Do you have news?" I asked. "Have the Japanese surrendered?"

She shook her head. "Not yet. But they've found George. He's alive! He was captured in Singapore, and taken to a prisoner of war camp, but he managed to escape, and join up with some freedom fighters, which joined forced with some of the American troops, so he gave them a letter to send home for him. He doesn't know when he'll be coming home, he says, but it can't be long now. The war will end soon, won't it?" She clutched her handkerchief with a white knuckled grip that spoke of desperation I think we all shared.

"It has to end," I said, and somehow it came out more certain than I felt.

Enough for Lucy to nod, wish me farewell, and head out into the evening light to catch the train home.

Inside the house, I found Captain Green's things were gone, including the army-issue blanket. All that was left on the bare mattress was a letter addressed to Captain McGregor.

I tore the envelope open, and a single folded sheet spilled out.

I began to read:

Dear Mrs McGregor

By the time you find this letter, the surrender should be signed, and you will soon be a civilian again, so I hope you do not mind that I address you as such.

I thank you for your kind hospitality during my time in Fremantle, and I hope you enjoy the use of this Harley Davidson motorcycle, in lieu of rent.

There is only one more thing I promised, and I am a man of my word.

You have a place reserved on a flying boat leaving for Potshot first thing in the morning. From there, you have a seat reserved on one of the planes headed to West Island, Cocos, where an airport is being constructed. I wish you a pleasant flight home, and I hope you find your family well.

If you ever feel the desire to see the Pacific Ocean or visit the United States, I would be delighted to offer you my hospitality in return. You will find my home address at the end of this letter.

I remain, respectfully and affectionately yours,

Douglas Green.

The letter is now tucked away inside my grandfather's chest, locked in the bunker beneath my garage, along with all the other belongings I'd found in Merry's house. My travelling trunks that had sailed on the *Islander* without me, the day William died, sat beside Dubhan's chest, still filled with books I hoped one day to read again, when I returned to Fremantle.

For return I would, when Apalala was old enough. Though, as I look at my daughter now, already a head taller than the last time I saw her, that might be sooner than I expect.

The war forced her to grow up faster than I would have wished, but it has changed us all. At least none of my people lost their lives to this war, though there were injuries. Machine gun fire damages siren flesh just as readily as the flesh of humans, and Apalala had already shown her aptitude as a healer in dressing our people's wounds.

I would not be surprised if she finds her calling as a healer. First in the ways of our people, and then perhaps using human medicine, when she is old enough to pay a visit to Merry's house in Fremantle.

But not yet. For we have been apart long enough, and the war is over. For now, I mean to take a moment to rejoice at being reunited with my family, for one day, war will come again, and next time, we will be ready.

ABOUT THE AUTHOR

Demelza Carlton has always loved the ocean, but on her first snorkelling trip she found she was afraid of fish.

She has since swum with sea lions, sharks and sea cucumbers and stood on spray drenched cliffs over a seething sea as a seven-metre cyclonic swell surged in, shattering a shipwreck below.

Demelza now lives in Perth, Western Australia, the shark attack capital of the world.

The *Ocean's Gift* series was her first foray into fiction, followed by her suspense thriller *Nightmares* trilogy. She swears the *Mel Goes to Hell* series ambushed her on a crowded train and wouldn't leave her alone.

Want to know more? You can follow Demelza on Facebook, Twitter, YouTube or her website, Demelza Carlton's Place at:

www.demelzacarlton.com

More Books by Demelza Carlton

<u>Colony: Holiday series</u>

Cowboys and Aliens (#1)

Ghost (#2)

Vulcan (#3)

Cupid (#4)

Valentine(#5)

Prometheus (#6)

<u>**Colony: Aqua series**</u>

Halcyon (#1)

Poseidon (#2)

Apollo (#3)

<u>**Siren of Secrets series**</u>

Ocean's Secret (#1)

Ocean's Gift (#2)

Ocean's Infiltrator (#3)

<u>**Siren of War series**</u>

Ocean's Justice (#1)

Ocean's Widow (#2)

Ocean's Bride (#3)

Ocean's Rise (#4)

Ocean's War (#5)

How To Catch Crabs

<u>**Nightmares Trilogy**</u>

Nightmares of Caitlin Lockyer (#1)

Necessary Evil of Nathan Miller (#2)

Afterlife of Alana Miller (#3)

<u>**Mel Goes to Hell series**</u>

The Devil's Work (#1)

See You in Hell (#2)

Mel Goes to Hell (#3)

To Hell and Back (#4)

The Holiday From Hell (#5)

All Hell Breaks Loose (#6)

The Devil Goes to Heaven (#7)

<u>**Romance Island Resort series**</u>
Maid for the Rock Star (#1)
The Rock Star's Email Order Bride (#2)
The Rock Star's Virginity (#3)
The Rock Star and the Billionaire (#4)
The Rock Star Wants A Wife (#5)
The Rock Star's Wedding (#6)
Maid for the South Pole (#7)

Romance a Medieval Fairytale series

Enchant: Beauty and the Beast Retold

Dance: Cinderella Retold

Fly: Goose Girl Retold

Revel: Twelve Dancing Princesses Retold

Silence: Little Mermaid Retold

Awaken: Sleeping Beauty Retold

Embellish: Brave Little Tailor Retold

Appease: Princess and the Pea Retold

Blow: Three Little Pigs Retold

Return: Hansel and Gretel Retold

Wish: Aladdin Retold

Melt: Snow Queen Retold

Spin: Rumpelstiltskin Retold

Kiss: Frog Prince Retold

Reflect: Snow White Retold

Roar: Goldilocks Retold

Cobble: Elves and the Shoemaker Retold

Float: Enchanted Horse Retold

Steal: Forty Thieves Retold

Call: Pied Piper Retold

Fall: Scheherazade Retold

Feather: Swan Maidens Retold

Curse: Rose Red Retold

Cross: Billy Goats Gruff Retold

Weave: Rapunzel Retold

Claim: Puss in Boots Retold

www.ingramcontent.com/pod-product-compliance
Lightning Source LLC
Chambersburg PA
CBHW070635170726
48291CB00003B/1027